MW00528149

THE
HIDDEN SEAL
OF THE REALM

THE
HIDDEN SEAL
OF THE REALM

A RICHARD HALLIBURTON ADVENTURE

BOOK 3

GARRETT DRAKE

The Hidden Seal of the Realm
© Copyright 2019 Garrett Drake

All rights reserved. No part of this book may be reproduced or transmitted in any form or by any means, electronic or mechanical, including photo-copying, recording, or by any information storage and retrieval system, without the written permission of the Publisher, except where permitted by law.

This book is a work of fiction. Any references to historical events, real people, or real locales are used fictitiously. Other names, characters, places, and incidents are products of the author's imagination, and any re-semblance to actual events or locales or persons, living or dead, is entirely coincidental.

First Print Edition 2020

Published in the United States of America

Green E-Books
PO Box 140654
Boise, ID 83714

For Mel, for his constant
encouragement and his infectious laugh

"We are born strangers in a strange land, and remain so. Travel simply reminds us of this essential truth. The transmission of a powerful story, one human to another, is an alchemical activity in which we are enlarged and changed."

— *Richard Halliburton*

PROLOGUE

January 11, 937 A.D.
Luoyang, China

EMPEROR LI CONGKE HIKED UP HIS ROBE AS HE RACED along the wall of his fortress. He stopped to survey the situation down below, hoping that his fortunes had changed. They hadn't. While a handful of his loyal soldiers fought valiantly, he cringed at the thought that their deaths would be in vain. Their sacrifices would amount to nothing, especially after he did what he was about to do.

He paced around the terrace just off his living quarters, considering if he had any other options.

"Sir, they've just breached the gates," one of the soldiers said.

Congke sighed and looked skyward. "Save yourself, Wang. And tell your fellow warriors to do the same. There's no use in you dying needlessly."

Wang shook his head. "That's not an option for us. We fight to the death."

"Whose death?" Congke asked. "Mine or yours?"

"Is there something you're trying to tell me?"

"This will all be over very soon, and I'd prefer that you were all still living once it was."

"But, sir, that's not what we do. No one expected a life of comfort and safety once we agreed to serve in your army."

9

"You also didn't expect to obey the orders of a coward."

Wang scowled. "Sir, you're not a coward. You're a—"

"I'm a coward," Congke said. "And that's an official decree, so don't try to argue with me."

"Did your decree get the holy seal of approval with it?"

Congke nodded as a faint smile appeared on his lips. "It's a message that arrived directly from heaven."

"I need to see the seal."

Congke dug into his pocket and pulled out the jade stone. He inspected it for a moment before tossing it to the soldier.

"This is the heirloom seal of the realm?" Wang asked.

The emperor nodded.

"And what am I supposed to do with this?"

"Give it to Ru Shi," Congke said. "Tell her that I wish I could do more, but there is no time."

"You want me to give this to her now? Right as the castle is about to be overrun?"

"This is the only opportunity I have to give it to her before it's either stolen or lost."

Wang cocked his head to one side. "And what is she supposed to do with this?"

"Trust me. She'll know."

"Whatever you desire, your majesty," the soldier said.

"Excellent. Now has all the treasure been secured?"

"Every last gold coin has been seal in the vault."

"Thank you for your service," Congke said. "Now consider yourself free, Wang."

* * *

WANG CLUTCHED THE STONE as he spun and raced away from the emperor's room where all his family had gathered. Stopping to take one last look, Wang affirmed his suspicions when he saw Congke and the rest of his family ascend the stairs to the tower.

With combatants pouring in, Wang looked like a common court hand as he dodged the men wielding swords. He wasn't sure he'd be able to locate Ru Shi in all the chaos, but he had to try. Congke was about to die, and Wang wanted to do everything in his power to honor the emperor's final request.

Wang navigated through the soldiers streaming through the gates and exited the castle. Across the street from the gate sat a young woman, her beauty unmatched by anyone he'd ever laid eyes on.

Ru Shi.

Wang hustled across the street, her gaze meeting his. He had to force himself to look away, despite the violent sword fights still being waged in the road.

"The emperor wanted you to have something," Wang said as he reached into his pocket. He retrieved the jade stone from his pocket and placed it in Ru Shi's hands.

"What is this?" she asked.

"The emperor said you would know and know what to do with it."

"It's the heirloom seal of the realm," she said. "It's the stamp of approval from the gods above."

"And what are you supposed to do with it?" he asked.

She smiled. "Would you like to see for yourself?"

He nodded.

"I thought you might. But you need to come with me. We need to make a little trip."

Ru Shi reached for his hand and took it, her soft skin caressing him.

"Where are we going?" he asked.

"Just be patient. You'll see soon enough."

Ru Shi glanced over her shoulder as a sword-wielding attacker leaped from a nearby ledge and drove his blade right through her heart. As the man straddled her dying body triumphantly, Wang drove his small knife into the man's neck. In a matter of seconds, he was gone.

Wang turned his attention toward Ru Shi, who was gasping for air as blood gushed from her body.

"I'm sorry," Wang said as he held her hand. "I tried to help you, I really did. So, before you go, tell me where this goes."

Ru Shi gasped for air as she tried to speak.

"It's all right," Wang said. "I'll figure it out."

In her eyes, Ru Shi seemed relieved—or maybe it was a cry for help. Wang couldn't tell much of a difference in his current state of survival.

"Run," she said.

Ru Shi's body fell limp as her hand opened up, the seal trickling through her fingers and onto the floor.

Wang looked over his shoulder and dove to his right just in time to avoid an oncoming blade. He rolled across the ground before bouncing to his feet and taking Ru Shi's advice to heart.

Wang sprinted away from the castle. Despite his lungs burning, he didn't stop until ten minutes had passed. When he did, he looked back at the fortress and noticed the tower just off the emperor's room was ablaze. Agonizing screams emanated from the fire. Just outside the door on the terrace leading to the tower, Wang could see a handful of soldiers ready to rush into the room and put an end to Congke's life if he hadn't succeeded on his own.

Seconds later, Congke, engulfed in flames, tumbled out of the tower and fell to the earth with a thud.

Wang glanced at the stone in his hand with no idea what Congke intended for it. But it didn't matter now. All that he cared about was carrying out the emperor's final order and making sure the jade stone was safe and secure, out of the hands of the enemy.

And Wang wasn't going to disappoint his master.

CHAPTER 1

RICHARD HALLIBURTON FINGERED THE PIECE OF COLD steel in his pocket as he sprinted down the hallway, wishing he was holding a gun instead of a Japanese cipher. There wasn't anyone to impede his path, which resulted in the same favorable conditions for the man trailing only a few yards behind. As Richard approached an intersection, he darted to the right and through a set of doors leading to the stairwell.

Taking the steps two at a time, he ascended to the roof and positioned himself behind the door to await the arrival of the Japanese spy. Richard crouched low and prepared to surprise the man by tackling him low and slamming him backward. As more time passed, Richard grew tenser. He was certain the operative was trailing close behind and wouldn't have needed more than a few seconds to catch up.

This is the last time I'll believe anyone who tells me an assignment is an easy one.

Richard eyed the handle carefully and waited for it to budge just the slightest alerting for him to jump the pursuing agent. After another minute elapsed, Richard scanned the rest of the roof. He turned his head slowly and stopped when he felt the barrel of a pistol pressed hard against his neck.

"On your feet," the man said.

Richard raised his hands in a posture of surrender and stood. The man stepped back, keeping his gun trained on Richard.

"What were you doing in my room?" the man asked. "What did you take?"

"Would you believe that I stayed there a few nights ago and had dropped my wedding ring underneath the bed?" Richard asked as he turned around to face the man.

"Is this a joke to you?"

Richard shook his head. "I was just doing my job."

"And what was your job?"

"To get your encryption key."

The spy eyed Richard carefully. "You're an American."

"You are quite astute. What gave me away? Was it my clothes? My accent? My devilishly good looks?"

"On your knees," the agent commanded.

Richard eyed the rest of the roof as he slowly descended, his hands still raised. "Look, I don't know who you are or quite frankly even care. If you let me go, I promise I won't follow you."

The man smirked. "I'm going to execute you and send a message to your superiors."

"My superiors don't even know that I'm doing this," Richard said. "It was just a favor for a friend."

"A favor? Stealing a cipher is a favor?" the spy said as he chuckled. "I don't believe you."

Richard shrugged. "It's your choice not to believe me, but if you shoot me now, you'll never know who's really after you."

"I already know."

Richard sighed and shook his head. "There's always more to the story."

"Enough. I'm done talking with you."

"Don't you want your cipher back?" Richard asked, stalling for time to think of a way to negotiate himself out of the situation.

"I'll collect it from your pocket after I shoot you," the agent said as he steadied his weapon with both hands.

"It's not in my pocket," Richard said. "If you kill me now, you're going to have a difficult time tracking it down. Not to mention everyone will be wondering why there's a dead body on top of this hotel."

"You think I'm going to leave you here?" the man asked with a chuckle. "No, I'm going to drag your body out to sea and let the fish feed on your rotting flesh."

"And that cipher you want so badly—you'll never find it."

"We're done talking," the spy said.

"If you're really going to kill me, couldn't you at least do the professional courtesy of giving me one last smoke?" Richard asked as he glanced at the pocket on his coat. "It's right in here if you'll allow me to retrieve it. I promise no funny business."

"No, that's not going to happen. Keep your hands where they are."

"Aren't you at least curious where I hid the cipher?" Richard asked.

"You're just going to tell me?" the agent asked. "If you're feeling so generous, of course I'd love to hear it before I kill you."

Richard grimaced and then sighed. "There's just one thing."

"What's that?"

Before Richard could answer, the spy collapsed to the ground beneath the crushing blow to the side of his skull. He hit the ground hard and didn't move.

Richard scrambled to his feet and drew back, keeping his hands in the air.

The woman standing over the Japanese agent looked at him and smiled, proud of her pistol-whipping prowess that felled him. She kicked his gun aside before turning her attention to Richard.

"Thank you," Richard said. "Look, I don't want any trouble. I just—"

"Can it," she said. "That's what partners do."

Richard lowered his hands and furrowed his brow. "Partners? I thought I was supposed to team up with someone else."

"Who?" she asked. "Agent Williams?"

He nodded slowly. "Yeah, I was told we would meet in the lobby later this evening and—"

She offered her hand. "Agent Williams," she said. "Agent Helen Williams."

"You're—you're not who I was expecting," he said, taking her hand.

"What's the matter? Haven't you ever seen a woman spy before?" she asked with a wink.

"No, it's just that—"

"Look, you need to learn to keep a lower profile instead of demanding everyone's attention on the dance floor. A good spy blends in, not cut a rug like Fred Astaire."

"I know," he said. "But when the music starts, I sometimes can't help myself."

"Well, now that I'm here, maybe I can rescue you from your inhibitions. Besides, the best way to go undercover anywhere is to pose as a couple. Nobody expects a woman to be prowling around as an intelligence officer for the U.S. Army. Uncle Sam will barely let women sit behind a desk to type up reports, much less run around in the shadows playing cloak and dagger."

"But here you are," Richard said.

She nodded and smiled. "Yes, here I am, a product of Hank Foster's rebellion against the policymakers. Or maybe he's just shrewder than anyone else in the spy game. Either way, the end result is all I care about."

The Japanese agent lunged toward Helen, but Richard noticed just in time. He stepped toward the man and delivered a teeth-rattling kick to the face, sending the operative back down to the ground and knocking him out.

"Thanks," Helen said as she bent down and grabbed his feet. "Want to give me a hand here?"

Richard took the agent's arms and followed Helen, who was lugging him toward the edge of the roof.

"Are you just going to throw him off?" Richard asked.

"How long have you been at this job?" she asked. "Haven't you figured out by now that it's far easier to let everyone believe he committed suicide than trying to dispose of a dead body?"

"Well, killing someone is usually the last option for me. I prefer to—"

"Your preference will get you more enemies than you could handle," she said. "The good thing about dead people is that they can only haunt you from the grave if you let them, but they'll never be able to hurt you. Now, on three."

Richard glanced over the edge to see if anyone was on the sidewalk below. Fortunately, the area was clear.

"One, two, three," Helen said.

Both of them released the body once it reached the apex of the swing and stepped forward to watch the spy smash against the hard ground.

"See how easy that was?" she asked.

Richard sighed. "We could've gotten more information

out of him if he was still alive."

"But he's not our assignment, which begs the question: What you were doing up here engaged with a Japanese operative?"

"Well, I—it's not exactly something I planned to do," Richard said. "It just kind of happened."

He dug into his pocket and produced a cipher.

"Whoa," she said. "Where'd you get that?"

"From his hotel room earlier today while I was helping out a fellow British agent."

"But you work for U.S. Army Intelligence, do you not?"

"It's a long story."

Helen folded her arms. "Let's hear it."

"Well, the short version is that this British spy I met named Ashenden had also been following the Reichswehr unit, compiling intelligence reports on their movements across Africa and Asia. Hank Foster told me to meet with this man and that he would share any recent findings with me about the Reichswehr's plans in China."

"And did he?" Helen asked.

"Not exactly, at least, not yet," Richard said. "He told me he'd tell me everything in exchange for a simple favor."

"Breaking into a Japanese spy's hotel room and stealing his cipher?" she said as she shook her head. "That's far from an easy task, even for a highly experienced agent, which you clearly are not."

"Now, now. You don't have to be so harsh. I know I'm relatively new to this profession, but I've already had some successful missions."

"That Reichswehr unit is still marching to China, isn't it?" she asked without waiting for a reply. "Then that means you weren't successful."

"Nobody ordered me to wipe out an entire unit.

Besides, that's going to draw exactly the kind of scrutiny that Army Intelligence doesn't want. I'm supposed to foil their plans, not eliminate them altogether."

"That's not any plan for success."

Richard shrugged. "Well, if we can keep them under surveillance, we'll at least know where they're going and what they're doing. If we eliminate them, the Germans will start over with a group of new agents, and we'll spend months playing catch up."

"Perhaps, but your Houdini act isn't sustainable. There will come a time when you won't have someone sneak up behind your would-be killer and bash him in the head."

"I'm sure you're right, but I must confess that the look on his face at the moment of impact was incredible," Richard said. "And while I'm sure I'm not long for this earth, I'm going to see as much of it as I can filled with as much adventure and peril as possible."

Helen's eyes widened. "You're insane."

"Congratulations, you're part of a long list of people who've told me that, though usually I only get that from people once I've told them what I plan to do on my travels. So, you're the first one to tell me that before I divulged all my deepest dreams as I gallivant across the planet."

"I'm afraid I'm going to regret this question," she said, followed by a slight sigh, "but what are your plans during your adventures?"

"Well, for starters, I'd like to swim the entire length of the Panama Canal," he said.

"Now that is lunacy," she said. "Are you aware that those waters are infested with crocodiles?"

"So I've heard, but I do have a plan for that."

"Spare me the details. I see why everyone calls you crazy."

Richard cocked his head to one side and eyed her carefully. "You're already dismissing me with that. I'm just getting started."

"No, you're not. I'm just an astute observer. And that was all I needed to hear to get the full picture."

"But—"

"You can tell me about it later, maybe after I've had a few drinks and will be more inclined to listen to your fanciful notions. In the meantime, we need to find that British spy of yours and get all the information he promised. I think it's safe to say you've more than fulfilled your obligation to him."

"That sounds like a plan to me," Richard said. "I'm supposed to meet him tonight at the Raffles Hotel bar around nine o'clock."

Helen turned and walked away. "I'll see you there then," she said as she strode toward the stairwell.

Richard waited until Helen disappeared before he reached into his other pocket and pulled out a message he'd found in the Japanese spy's briefcase. He unfolded it and placed it on the ground began deciphering the note. After a couple of minutes, the full note became clear, and Richard's eyes widened.

What could've been so important that Ashenden would've been willing to pass this assignment to me?

Richard hustled down the steps. He needed to send a message to Hank Foster.

CHAPTER 2

RICHARD SLUNG HIS COAT OVER HIS SHOULDER AS HE sauntered up to the famed Raffles Hotel bar, which seemed to stretch all the way into the South China Sea. He scanned the patrons briefly before identifying the lone man sitting at the near corner, puffing a cigar.

"How's your evening going, sir?" Richard asked once he came to a stop next to the man.

"Better than your afternoon," Ashenden said after shooting a glance at Richard. "That was quite a mess you made out there today."

Richard settled into the seat next to the British agent and ordered a drink before responding. "That's not how I intended for things to go."

"I told you it was a simple assignment," Ashenden said as he stared at the bottom of his empty glass. "If I thought for one second that you were going to kill that agent, I would've never asked you to help me."

"There was nothing simple about it," Richard said, "especially when the operative returned to his room and caught me red-handed. I didn't have much of a choice."

"You could've portrayed yourself as a burglar and just grabbed anything of value lying around. He would've likely dismissed the incident as something that just happens when you're traveling in Singapore."

"He saw me digging through his suitcase."

"So you led him to the top floor and threw him over the ledge?"

Richard sighed. "That's not exactly how it went down. He was about to kill me when a fellow agent lent me a hand."

Helen eased onto the stool next to Ashenden. He tried to ignore, but he kept glancing back at her as she took his hand and started caressing it.

"Miss, I'm sorry, but I'm in the middle of a conversation here," Ashenden said. "Would you mind finding another seat along the bar?"

"Why? So you can divulge valuable information without me around?" she asked.

Ashenden furrowed his brow and drew back. "Excuse me. Who exactly are you?"

Richard leaned in close to Ashenden. "That's my fellow agent, the one who saved me, and the one whose idea it was to toss the Japanese agent's body off the top of the hotel."

"A woman agent?" he asked, his eyes widening. "Why I never—"

"Heard of such a thing?" Helen said with a wry smile. "It's maddening, isn't it? You let us start voting and the next thing you know, we're working alongside you instead of organizing your paperwork."

"To be quite frank, I'm less bothered by that than I am by your reckless behavior and hurling one of the most important spies in the Japanese empire to his death," Ashenden said. "Not only did we need him to be alive, but his next actions would also help us determine what he knew about the militaries of the western world. It was vital that he used our cipher to transmit a few messages. And now that opportunity is gone. Months and months of work out the window—or in this case, off the roof. Not to mention that

I'll likely be a prime suspect in his death and raise the ire of the Kenpeitai."

"Well, aren't you just full of sunshine," she said. "I'm sure you'll be able to dodge them, just like you dodged this assignment."

Ashenden scowled. "What is the meaning of this? If you still want me to share that vital intelligence with you, I suggest you stop insinuating such lies."

Richard shrugged. "It is curious that you sought my help on such an important assignment, albeit one you deemed so simple. What could've possibly trumped getting your hands on this pivotal piece of spycraft?"

He slipped the cipher into Ashenden's hand, which he inspected only after scanning the room twice.

"Messiness aside, you succeeded in getting this for me," Ashenden said as he studied the object. "And for that, I am grateful. It will hamper our efforts in the distant future, but for now, it should yield a treasure trove of information."

"Speaking of information, isn't it about time that you finally delivered on your promise since I upheld my end of the bargain?" Richard asked.

Ashenden inspected his cigar for a moment before tapping the ashes into a tray. "Let's go to my room where it's more private so we can talk."

Richard and Helen followed Ashenden out of the bar and up to the second floor. He led them to his room and closed the door behind them before continuing.

"Please," he said, gesturing to the two chairs near the window, "have a seat."

"I appreciate the discretion," Richard said. "We obviously can't be too careful around here, can we?"

Ashenden shook his head. "There's a ship called the *Minerva*, which leaves here once a week. It's the same ship that a group of Reichswehr soldiers boarded last week to set off for China."

"We'd already heard China was the next location the Germans were targeting for a potential archeological dig," Richard said. "We were hoping to get the kind of intelligence we could act upon."

"Patience," Ashenden said. "I'm getting to that. However, I must let you know upfront that this isn't the same kind of mission you might have embarked upon in the past when it pertained to this Reichswehr unit."

Richard's eyebrows shot upward. "And why's that?"

"This is more of a search than a dig," Ashenden said. "The Germans are searching for the lost Heirloom Seal of the Realm, which is worth a fortune and an artifact long sought after by the ruling dynasties in China."

"What's so special about this seal?" Richard asked.

Ashenden drained the remaining liquid in his glass. "Supposedly, if you possessed this seal as an emperor, it meant that whatever you decreed was endorsed by the deities, straight from the mouth of God."

"And how much is this artifact worth?" Helen asked.

"It's all just speculating at this point, but antiquities experts believe it will fetch a half million pounds. However, who knows what the prevailing rulers of China would pay to have that long lost item in the country's treasury."

Richard stared out the window, lost in thought. He had plenty of questions about the seal, and he wasn't sure where to begin.

"What are you thinking?" Helen asked him.

Richard shook his head. "For starters, I'm wondering why all of a sudden there is such a renewed interest in this heirloom seal. I mean, why now? It's been lost for nearly a thousand years, but out of the blue it becomes this sought after piece. It's odd."

Ashenden shrugged. "Not if you consider that there have been plenty of rumors heating up from the archeological experts that the seal is still out there and that several of them believe they know where it is."

"Again, why now?" Richard asked. "What new information has come to light that makes this pursuit more attainable, or at least gives all these excavators hope that they can find it?"

"A French archeologist named Jean Renault published an article about his findings several months ago that's responsible for stoking this interest," Ashenden said. "He unearthed some papers from the twelfth century that suggested the seal was still around then. For a long time, the seal was believed to be lost when Emperor Mo of the Later Tang dynasty committed suicide with his family by retreating to a tower in his fortress and setting fire to it when his army was under attack. After that event in history, the seal was never again mentioned by any ruling dynasties. However, Renault found something that suggested the seal was being hidden by a group who had suffered greatly due to the previous emperor's abuse of the seal."

"And now everyone is trying to find it," Helen said.

"Exactly," Ashenden said. "And the country is now teeming with archeologists ready to ram their shovels into the ground and claim their prize."

"So, where is everybody looking?" Richard asked.

"All over the country," Ashenden said. "There doesn't seem to be much consensus on where the seal is now. However, that's not entirely surprising given the egos of all these experts eager to stake a claim to their foreknowledge of the location. It's all a game to enhance their reputation among the universities."

"Unless they're far more interested in selling a piece of history for hundreds of thousands of pounds than they are achieving notoriety for it," Helen said. "There are some people who care about prominence and others who care about wealth."

"You have a good point," Ashenden said. "However, I have it on good authority that Renault omitted the evidence he gathered pointing toward the seal's location in the southeast part of the country and likely near Canton."

"That would make sense," Helen said. "If the *Minerva* is headed into port at Hong Kong, Canton isn't that far away."

Ashenden looked at Helen and held his gaze for a moment. "Your knowledge of China's geography is impressive. Have you spent much time there?"

"More than I care to recall," she said. "It's the far east's version of the wild west."

"I'm surprised you made it out alive," Ashenden said. "I prefer to avoid that country at all costs, though sometimes duty requires it."

"We all make sacrifices," Helen said. "Now, is there anything else we need to know about this seal?"

Ashenden shook his head. "That's all I know. Go to Canton and start looking for Germans—or the seal. Either way, you're going to be inviting trouble."

Richard chuckled. "Trouble finds me wherever I am, whether on a simple assignment or wading into a den of thieves. But adventure also ensues." His eyes twinkled as he glanced at Helen.

"Almost getting killed is not an adventure you should be excited about," Helen said.

Ashenden nodded. "She's right. You need to be very careful, or you'll be buried in that godforsaken country—if you're lucky."

"Without danger, there is no adventure," Richard said, wagging his finger at Ashenden. "Thanks for the information on the Germans and the seal. I'm sure our paths will cross soon."

Helen left first with Richard trailing right behind her.

"That guy's an interesting fellow," Helen said. "I hope he's on our side."

"Why do you say that?"

"The stunt he pulled sending you after that cipher—he never even answered your question about why he couldn't do it himself."

"I'm sure there was a reason. You should know well enough by now that you don't always give a straight answer when asked something you'd rather keep to yourself."

"Yeah, but there's something else about that guy. I just can't put my finger on it."

"Well, if you already felt that way about that agent, I guess there's no harm in showing you this," Richard said as he stopped and fished the piece of paper out of his pocket. "I found this and translated it using the Japanese decryption key. What do you think?"

Helen's eyebrows shot upward as she perused the translation Richard had scrawled next to the original note. "Are you sure this is authentic?"

"I don't know why it wouldn't be."

Her gaze remained on the page. "Have you told Hank about this?"

"Not yet."

"Well, you need to first thing in the morning," she said. "Now, get to your room and pack. We've got a ship to catch tomorrow at noon."

CHAPTER 3

RICHARD BOARDED THE MINVERVA AND SEARCHED FOR his quarters. His ticket listed his name as Maxwell Harrington, while Helen was going by Margaret. He reached down and took her hand, squeezing it and flashing her a faint smile.

"I believe your suite is this way, Mr. Harrington," the porter said gesturing for his guests to follow him.

Richard matched the room number on his boarding pass with the one affixed to the door.

"Do we have a match?" the porter asked.

Richard nodded. "It appears that we do."

"Excellent," the porter said. "I'll leave you two to get settled in."

Richard pressed a coin into the man's hand before he scurried down the corridor to usher in the next set of guests.

"Two beds?" Helen asked. "Aren't we supposed to be married?"

Richard shrugged. "I need my space."

"And here I was thinking you were just a perfect gentleman."

"I didn't think I needed any more proof in that department," Richard said with a grin. "I would've thought my actions conveyed that by now. I didn't realize you needed further proof."

"My father always told me that when things seemed too good to be true, it's because they probably were."

Richard picked up a brochure on the dresser, ignoring Helen as she continued to go on about Richard's credibility as a "swell chap."

"Helen, would you look at this?" Richard asked as he held the paper only a few inches from her face. "They're having a ship-wide dance competition tonight."

"And you're thinking about going?"

Richard nodded. "Of course, especially since there's a grand prize of ten pounds to the winner. That should be enough to get me a nice upgrade on one of my upcoming trips. You do understand how dreadful it is to stay in the coach cabins. The lack of sleep, the noise, the smells. It's just not any way to travel."

"I will pay you twenty pounds not to go on the dance floor," she said. "It's not worth risking our cover. You never know who might be lurking aboard this ship. Perhaps one of your many enemies or someone Karl Wilhelm sent back to Singapore to kill you. It's just not worth it."

"Now that you put it that way—I'm most definitely going to participate. The added element of danger makes this all the more alluring to me."

Helen scowled as she cocked her head to one side and stared slack-jawed at Richard. "Do you truly wish to die? Because if you do, I can save us a lot of trouble and dump your body once we get out to sea."

"No one's going to recognize me, Margaret," he said. "In fact, I would prefer that you join me out on the dance floor."

"That's not going to happen," she said.

"Shy about your dancing ability, are we?"

"Trust me when I say this, but that's the last thing I'm worried about while we're on this ship. I just want us to keep our heads down and act as if we're a normal couple on a regular holiday trip, just like everyone else. It shouldn't be that difficult."

"And a normal couple who could dance wouldn't shy away from kicking off their shoes and cutting a rug for the enjoyment of everyone else. Any man and woman who've been together for any significant amount of time wouldn't hesitate to share their talents with the rest of the world."

"I prefer that only a few select enemies of my country see my skills up close and personal—and it be the last thing they see, too."

Richard furrowed his brow. "Did you always have such blood lust?"

She shook her head. "Most of my life I didn't, but that was before I watched my father murdered by a German spy while he was serving as a diplomat there just before the war started."

"Oh, Helen, I'm so sorry. That must've been awful."

"It's Margaret," she said, wagging her finger at him as she reminded him to stay in disguise, even when they were alone. "You never know who's listening."

"And you never know who's watching," he said. "Perhaps this will be my opportunity to dance in front of a talent scout. I've always thought it would be fun to dance and sing in musicals on Broadway."

"Please tell me that you don't sing," she said.

"You, my dear, will fall asleep each night to my enchanting songs and—"

"Stop right there," she said. "Just remember that I sleep with my knife under my pillow. And I'm also prone to sleepwalking."

"Don't be such a spoilsport," Richard said. "Please dance with me tonight."

"Not a chance."

* * *

THE *MINERVA* CHUGGED out of the harbor an hour later and sliced through the choppy seas for the better part of the afternoon. Eventually, smoother waters prevailed, and all the guests gathered in the dining hall for that evening's dinner.

After the meal was completed, the ship's servants moved several tables around until a sizable area appeared in the middle of the room. Against the far wall, a band hurriedly set up and wasted no time playing a song to get everyone in the mood for a night of dancing.

"Everyone received a notice about the dance competition in your rooms earlier today when you checked in, right?" asked a man who paced back and forth near the band after it wrapped up its first song.

The crowd responded in a mumbled affirmation, spurring him to continue. He wore a long red sports coat with tails and a pair of white pants, accented by shiny black boots, a top hat, and a dark wooden cane. While he looked more like a carnival barker to Richard, the man's approach was effective as the room fell silent and everyone gave him their attention.

"Excellent," he said. "Now that we have that cleared up, it's time to explain the rules of this evening's festivities."

The emcee, who referred to himself as Mr. Underhill, spent the next five minutes detailing the process of how he and three hand-picked judges would determine the winner of the contest. Upon completion of the rules, Mr. Underhill invited the first guest who felt inclined to step onto the dance floor.

Richard raised his hand, which was promptly yanked down by Helen.

"What are you doing?" she asked. "Are you insane? I

thought we went over how you weren't going to participate in this competition, remember? Keep our heads down and blend in?"

"We must've interpreted your talk different," Richard said as he stood up. "Maxwell Harrington, here."

"Mr. Harrington, are you going to start this competition for us?" the emcee asked.

Richard nodded as a spotlight from the far side of the room fell on him while the rest of the lights went dark.

"Thank you for your courage, Mr. Harrington. We'll begin with the Foxtrot, which means I believe you'll need a partner."

"In that case, might I suggest my wife, Mrs. Margaret Harrington," Richard said as he shot a look over at her.

She sneered at him before standing up and plodding her way through the sea of chairs and tables until she joined him beneath a bright glare.

"You can do this," Richard said through his teeth. "Just follow my lead."

She smiled and rolled her eyes. "How about you see if you can keep up," she whispered.

Richard held out his hand for Helen as they sauntered toward the center of the room. He guided her to their starting position and waited for the music to begin. "Dapper Dan" was the selection played by the band, free of any lyrics. Richard and Helen glided back and forth to the movements of slow, quick, quick. As the song rollicked along, both of them had moments where they shined—Richard with his improvisation skills as he spun Helen around while keeping them moving to the beat; Helen with her fancy footwork that drew several oohs and ahhs from the onlookers. Once the song came to an end, the crowd erupted in applause.

"Ladies and gentlemen, who's possibly brave enough

to follow that?" Mr. Underhill asked.

A few awkward seconds passed before another couple volunteered.

"Way to blend in," Helen said with a sneer.

"I am," Richard said. "I'm just a passenger on a ship who happens to enjoy dancing. A spy would never even dare to enter a dance competition and probably win the event. But that's what makes me so different. I do what no one would expect an intelligence officer to do, thereby maintaining my unassuming position on this ship."

"We'll see about that."

Once all the people who felt so inclined to display their acumen for the foxtrot in front of strangers finished, Mr. Underhill announced the winner.

"Mr. and Mrs. Adams, would you please come over here to the podium to receive your trophy for winning tonight's competition," Underhill said.

Helen huffed a breath through her nose in disgust. "It's only because they went last. She wasn't half as good as me."

"What about me?" Richard asked, feigning offense.

Helen shrugged. "Mr. Adams had far more deft moves on the floor than you did."

"I know you're only saying that to get a rise out of me," Richard said. "Even the most neutral of observers could tell that my skills were considerably higher than that man's."

As the passengers began to disperse around the ship for late-night drinks and card games, Richard and Helen lingered at their table for a moment.

"You have to admit that we were pretty good together," Richard said.

"We're not hired as professional dancers," Helen said. "We're supposed to be gathering information and letting our superiors decide what to do with it."

"Or stopping someone from rebuilding their war chest and launching another assault on the world."

"That too," Helen said.

As they were about to get up, an elderly man shuffled toward them and held out his hand as he spoke. "Mr. and Mrs. Harrington, was it?"

Richard stood up and took the man's hand. "That's correct. And you are?"

"Tomas Diaz," he said as he turned and shook Helen's hand. "I just wanted to say that you should've won. You two were clearly the best dancers this evening. And if you had been the ones dancing last, I'm sure Mr. Underhill would've awarded you the grand prize."

Richard waved dismissively at the man. "You're too kind, sir."

"I speak the truth," Diaz said. "And I think deep down you probably know it."

"We appreciate the kind words," Helen said with a smile.

"And what brings you on this voyage, Mr. Diaz?" Richard asked.

"I'm an archeologist nearing the end of my time at the University of Paris, and I figured it was time I visited one of the sites I've always dreamed about and seeing if my theory is correct."

"And what location is that?"

"China," Diaz said with a wink. "You didn't really think I was going to give away decades of research to a complete stranger, did you?"

Richard shook his head. "Of course not. It's just that—"

"What my husband is trying to say is that he's simply wondering what you might be searching for in China," Helen said. "Sometimes he gets tongue-tied when in public. But it's also what I find so endearing about him. He can be full of himself behind closed doors, yet when you get him in public, he clams up."

Diaz winked at Richard. "I totally understand. I used to be the same way myself. Well, at least the part about not knowing how to speak in public. I still think very highly of myself."

"That's not what I—oh, never mind," Richard said.

"See what I mean," Helen said with a smile and glance at Diaz. "I appreciate you making the effort to tell us that, but I'm afraid we must be going."

"Xanadu," Diaz blurted out. "I'm going to Xanadu in search of a long lost treasure supposedly buried by pirates. Is your curiosity satisfied now?"

Richard laughed. "Sir, you didn't really have to tell us, but might I ask what made you change your mind?"

"You look harmless," Diaz said. "And digging is a task that requires precision. Not many people have what it takes."

"What if I told you we were headed to China to look for an ancient object as well?" Helen said.

"I'd say you completely fooled me," Diaz said. "And if you are, what exactly are you searching for?"

"The heirloom seal of the realm," Richard responded. "Are you familiar with it?"

Diaz shuddered. "I wouldn't touch that seal if forced to choose between it and thousands of dollars. It's cursed, I tell you."

"Cursed?" Richard said. "It's just a small jade stone used to stamp messages from the emperor."

"Trust me," Diaz said. "If you know what's good for you, you'll stay far away from that seal."

With that statement, Diaz eased around in the opposite direction and hobbled away, leaning on his cane. He looked down and shook his head as he vanished into the passengers milling around the dance floor.

"Now, if we hadn't have danced, would we have learned such valuable information about the heirloom seal?" Richard asked.

"You heard that gentleman," Helen said. "It's cursed."

"Of course it is," Richard said with a grin. "That only adds to the intrigue of this mission."

"We don't have to find it. We only have to stop the Reichswehr unit from stealing out of the country with it."

Richard couldn't stop smiling as he responded. "Either way, it would appear that we will have a tremendous challenge ahead of us—and I can't wait to find that seal."

CHAPTER 4

Macau

KARL WILHELM TIGHTENED HIS GLOVES AS HE PACED back and forth in the dimly lit hotel room. He shot a glance at his captive audience, the world-renowned French archeologist Jean Renault. Despite Renault's initial reluctance to consider Wilhelm's proposal, he knew that the proper incentive would sway the expert to at least listen to it. And if Renault was still unwilling to help the Reichswehr unit, there were always other methods to ensure full cooperation.

"There's absolutely no reason we shouldn't partner together," Wilhelm said as he stopped and faced Renault again. "We want different things that can only be accomplished by working together."

"That's no how I see it," Renault said. "This is not a venture I ever launched in hopes of making myself rich."

"Precisely my point," Wilhelm said, shooting a glance at his top commander Hans Reinhard, who stood silently in the corner of the room behind Renault. "You want notoriety over finding an object that's been lost for nearly a millennium. We want to sell the object."

"It's a piece of history, not a commodity to be bought and sold."

"Of course," Wilhelm said, "but someone has to pay for this expedition, don't they?"

Renault shrugged. "Sure, but my dig is already funded."

"What about when you run out of money? Or what if you don't have the manpower necessary to find the seal?"

"Well, I think that—"

"You're not thinking," Wilhelm said as he stamped his foot. "That's your problem. You haven't yet considered all the lost time you will incur if you attempt this project on your meager budget. And the longer you go without discovering the seal, the more your standing suffers among your colleagues."

"I'm staking my reputation on this expedition, so don't try to lecture me that I haven't considered every possible scenario here," Renault said as he narrowed his eyes. "That's exactly what I do every day. I look at all the possibilities based on the evidence and draw conclusions, careful to consider each variable and how it might affect my overall thesis. I wouldn't be doing this if I weren't confident I'd find the seal."

"And your confidence is why I believe you're the kind of person we're looking to work with," Wilhelm said.

"Perhaps I'm not making myself clear enough," Renault said as he rose from his chair. "I'm not interested in working with anyone. My team is competent and amply supplied. We are funded for two years, so I don't think we need your help. Now, if you'll excuse me, I must be going."

Renault took a couple of strides before Wilhelm placed his hand on the archeologist's chest. "Please reconsider."

"Get out of my way," Renault said, glaring at Wilhelm.

"Sit down," Wilhelm said. "We're not finished here."

"Are you holding me prisoner?"

Wilhelm removed his hand before snapping his fingers. "Hans, bring me the diary."

Renault's eyes widened. "Where did you get that?"

Wilhelm wagged his finger in Renault's face. "I think

the better question is where did you get this from? I happened to know that your colleagues might be interested in seeing this."

"You need to give that back to me right this instance," Renault said.

Wilhelm used his elbow to shield Renault's lunge for the book. He tried again before Reinhard placed his hands on Renault's shoulders and forced him back into his chair.

"This is yours, is it?" Wilhelm asked as he casually turned the pages. "I think the archeology community would be surprised that you take notes in English. And never mind the fact that your handwriting closely resembles that of Dr. Thurston Miller."

"What are you insinuating?" Renault asked. "Do you think I stole this from him?"

"It certainly does appear that way," Wilhelm said.

"He gave it to me because he feared someone was after him and would kill him to get their hands on his research notes. Now I have a good idea who it was."

"That's an interesting story. However, I also know that you were relatively unknown until you recently published this story on the heirloom seal of the realm. No major discoveries or findings to your name. Just a tired old professor. It seems far more likely that he feared someone like you, a failed archeologist desperate to achieve something with his life."

"That's a lie," Renault roared as he struggled to escape Reinhard's grasp. "Everyone who knows me would never believe such an accusation."

Wilhelm knelt in front of Renault to get eye level with him. "Despite what you might believe your friends think about you, deep down, everyone harbors distrust for others. All you have to do is provide people with a reason to believe it's true."

"I'll take my chances," Renault said as he grabbed for the diary.

Wilhelm jerked it back, keeping it just out of Renault's reach. "You think I'm just going to give this to you and let you walk out of here, especially after what I know about you?"

"If you don't—"

"Then what, Dr. Renault? You're going to tell the authorities that the Germans stole your notebook? The one you wrote meticulous details in English, no less. You and I both know that would end even more disastrously for you. It's one thing to die in anonymity, but it's another to live out the rest of your life in shame, which is what you'd be doing if you had the gall to report this. However, I have a proposal for you."

Renault pursed his lips. "I'm listening."

"Good boy," Wilhelm said as he patted Renault on the head. "Now, I think it's evident that we need each other. You need Dr. Miller's—I mean—your notebook to find the seal. We need the actual seal. We can do this together, which would be in both our best interests."

"And how does that work?"

"You would get credit for the discovery, cementing your fame in finding an artifact that had been lost for nearly a thousand years," Wilhelm said. "And then we would broker a deal with the highest bidder, collecting all the profits. Apart from each other, you would be relying on your memory and hoping that you could find it before funding ran out or we found it. And we would simply waste a lot of time finding another expert willing to work with us and decipher Dr. Miller's notes, time I'm not particularly interested in wasting. So, what do you say? Partners?"

Wilhelm offered his hand to Renault, who looked at it in disgust.

"I don't really have a choice, do I?" he asked.

"We always have a choice," Wilhelm said. "But we don't always get to choose the consequences of our actions. However, in this case, you do. Work together and become famous for more than simply writing an article that caused a stir in the archeological community. Work apart and die a failure and a disgraced thief."

"When you put it like that, I'll pass," Renault said as he stood up. "I'd rather die in disgrace than work with you. Now if you'll excuse me, I have work to do."

Wilhelm turned and nodded at Reinhard, who followed Renault out the door and down the street.

CHAPTER 5

Hong Kong
November 17, 1922

W HEN THE *MINERVA* PULLED INTO PORT JUST
before daybreak eight days later, Richard and Helen
wasted no time in exiting the ship. They
maneuvered their way along the bustling docks, dodging the
fishermen who were returning from a long night out on the
water. Richard's backpack snagged once, getting caught up in
a net while passing a deckhand. The faux pas resulted in a steely
glare from the captain as he led his crew toward the market.

Richard clasped his hands and bowed as he mouthed
the word "sorry" to the fishermen, who acknowledged the
apology by huffing and shaking their heads.

"What's wrong with those guys?" Richard asked. "By
the way, they were looking at me, you would've thought I
punched one of their sisters in the face."

Helen chuckled. "Welcome to Hong Kong. As you're
quickly learning, this isn't exactly a bastion of friendliness.
The people here aren't going to take to your affable nature
very easily."

"I find that hard to believe," Richard said as he tried to
keep pace with Helen. "And is there a reason you're
running?"

Helen maintained her pace and ignored Richard's
complaint. "Believe it. This part of your adventure will only

45

merit a few pages in your book, if that. It's not that this part of the world isn't interesting, but the people aren't interested in you. You'd have to stay here for a while to get them to warm up to you."

"I'm going to accept your challenge and prove you wrong."

"Be my guest, but you're only going to disappoint yourself."

They hustled along for another minute until Helen darted down one of the ramps toward an aging shrimping boat.

"How is that thing even floating?" Richard asked as he studied the rickety wooden vessel that was in desperate need of a fresh coat of paint along with major repairs on the main deck.

Helen shrugged as she stopped in front of the ship. "It's not really making many voyages these days. It's more of an office."

"An office?"

"Come on," she said, stepping aboard. "I'll show you."

Richard followed her, striding onto the deck and following Helen below.

"What are we doing here again?" he asked.

"We're gathering some information," she said. "But just let me do the talking, okay?"

"What are you afraid I'm going to say?"

"I never know—and that's the problem. I can't have you blurting out something stupid to someone like Yao Kai."

"Yao Kai? Is he our contact here in Hong Kong?"

"He's my contact, and he won't like the fact that you're simply here with me," Helen said. "I once saw him feed one of his men to a shark for insubordination."

"Sounds a bit harsh, don't you think?"

"You think you're funny, but trust me, nobody was laughing. And if you don't lighten up, he might jam a couple of fish hooks into you and yank you up off the deck."

"This doesn't sound like the kind of guy I want to be friends with."

"Better than being his enemy, trust me."

"Okay, I'll try to be quiet."

Helen strode up to the captain's quarters and nodded at the man who stood guard outside the door. He held up his hand and poked his head inside and said something before turning around.

"Mr. Kai will see you now," he said, swinging the door open wide. As Richard tried to follow Helen, the guard slid between them.

"He's with me," Helen said.

The guard shook his head. "Mr. Kai will only see you."

Helen spun and turned toward Kai, who was puffing on a pipe as he sat behind his desk. "Is this how you treat me after all the information I brought you the last time we met?"

Kai blew a smoke ring and shrugged before looking at his guard and signaling for him to let in Richard. As the man moved aside, Richard forced a smile and nodded. The door slammed hard behind them.

"Sorry, Helen," Kai said. "You know I only trust you."

"Well, this guy is harmless, unless you get into a dance competition with him," she said. "He's pretty nifty with his feet."

"Is he?" Kai asked as he stroked his beard. Before Richard could confirm his partner's claim, he watched Kai yank open a desk drawer and pull out a gun. He trained it on Richard for a moment before pointing it at his feet and firing a shot.

Richard leaped in the air, darting back and forth across the room.

"What's the meaning of this?" Richard asked.

Kai squeezed off another shot before leaning back in his chair and breaking into a maniacal laugh.

"That's not funny," Helen said.

"You're right, Helen," Kai said. "He's quite the dancer."

"You don't have to shoot at me to get me to dance," Richard said. "A radio or a record player—two certain ways to get me moving without firing a weapon, unless you just like to make people nervous."

Kai rose to his feet and aimed his gun at Richard again. "That's my specialty."

After a few tense seconds, Kai pulled the trigger.

Click.

No gunshot followed, just the hollow and empty sound of a chamber firing without a round inside. Kai broke into uproarious laughter.

"You're crazy," Richard said.

"I've been called worse," Kai said. "Much, much worse. But I prefer the Hong Kong Head Hunter. And who knows? Maybe you're next."

Richard sighed while Kai flashed a toothy grin.

"I'm just having fun with you," Kai said as eased around the side of his desk and slapped Richard on the back. "You seem like someone who could take a joke."

"Those aren't exactly the kind of jokes I find very humorous."

"What I find humorous is that Helen brought you here, like there won't be consequences for her doing so."

Helen took a deep breath. "I don't really have a choice. We were thrust together as partners, and I can't leave him outside. If I didn't bring him in and let you meet him, your men would probably wonder what I'm doing with him. Better to make my intentions clear up front."

"So why are you here again?" Kai asked.

"Nothing happens on these docks without you finding out about them. And we happen to need some information about a group of German soldiers who arrived a few days ago. Did you happen to hear about them?"

Kai strode around the room. "What is that information worth to you?"

"It's not just about what it's worth to us, but to you as well," Helen said. "They intend to steal a long lost Chinese artifact and resell it with the profits going toward rebuilding their country's military."

"And we should be afraid of the Germans?"

"They were the ones who started World War I," Richard said, taking advantage of every opportunity to break into the conversation. "But we understand that they are planning on an encore. And we're certain it'd be one that was far more destructive than their first one."

"Okay," Kai said. "I'll tell you what you want to know about them."

Helen settled into a seat across from Kai's desk, while Richard remained standing against the back wall.

"I'm ready," she said. "What do you know?"

"There were a dozen of them," Kai answered. "And they were all supposedly heading to Macau."

"Macau?" she asked as she furrowed her brow.

"Yes, they are after some artifact like you said, though I never heard what it was so I can't confirm what I believe they're seeking. I just know that they were dangerous looking, though nothing my men wouldn't be able to handle."

"Looks can be deceiving," Richard said. "I can attest to the fact that they are a fierce bunch."

"Personally?" Kai said, raising an eyebrow. "That must mean that you've had a run-in with them—and lived."

Richard nodded.

Kai grinned and gestured toward Richard as he addressed Helen. "This is how I know they aren't a serious threat. Even this man could escape them."

"I know you don't like him, Kai, but he's not a complete imbecile," Helen said. "Now is there anything else I should know?"

"As a matter of fact, there is," Kai said. "Don't waste your time following them. There's no way that seal is anywhere near where they were going."

"And how do you know this?" she asked.

"Because I belong to a secret society, and our job is to protect the seal."

Helen's eyes widened. "Wait, you know where the seal is?"

Kai nodded. "Why are you acting so surprised? Why do you think I have so many men? It takes plenty of trained warriors to protect such a secret."

"Why haven't you sold it to someone in the government?" she asked.

"That object isn't for sale—and if it were, I'd hunt down anyone who sought to profit from it. But that's why I'm not worried about those Germans. They have no idea where to look. If they did, I'd have them all gutted and use what was left of them as bait for one of my upcoming fishing expeditions."

"Anything else I should know?" Helen asked.

Kai cast a wary look at Richard. "Just keep an eye on that guy. He looks like trouble to me."

"Probably not in the way you're suggesting," she said with a smile, "but don't worry, I will."

Kai hugged Helen and politely kissed her on both cheeks before nodding at Richard.

"It was a pleasure meeting you," Richard said, forcing

a grin before he turned toward the door.

As Richard reached for the doorknob, a knife sank into the wood with a thud. He turned around slowly and saw Kai staring coldly.

"Better not let my Helen get hurt," he said. "I'll hold you personally responsible if anything happens to her. And I promise you that you don't want to let her get hurt."

"I wouldn't dream of it," Richard said before striding out of the room and heading toward the deck.

When Richard and Helen left the ship and were on the docks again, he stopped suddenly and faced her. "What was that back there?"

"What was what?" she asked.

"You seem more than willing to offer me up as fish bait for your buddy, Kai."

She chuckled. "Oh, Richard, you haven't spent much time in this part of the world or maybe even with miscreants anywhere. You have to tell them what they want to hear and be as loyal as possible. It's how I got some critical information, which is what we needed to know in order to bring an end to this quest by the Reichswehr."

"The only way we're going to bring this to an end is if we kill the entire Reichswehr unit, which everyone thinks is going to start another Great War," Richard said. "So we need another way."

"And have you already thought of an alternate plan?"

Richard nodded. "I have."

"And when did you do that?"

"When the two of you were playing kissy-face back there in his office. There was an idea that just dawned on me."

"For the record, I don't like Kai. He was just being polite. That's how people greet one another or say goodbye in this part of the world."

"Well, as much as I hate to admit it," Richard said, "I

think we need to take Kai's advice and forget about the Reichswehr for now. They're looking in the wrong place. So, we need to look in the right place and beat them to the seal. If we do that, we can get it in the hands of the right people, preventing any such sale on the black market."

Helen's mouth fell agape as she stared at Richard. "You really believed him, didn't you?"

"What exactly are you referring to?"

She smiled. "He told us that the Germans were looking in the wrong place—and you believed him."

"You think he's lying?"

"He's absolutely lying to us," she said. "That's what these type of men do. They lie straight to your face."

"How do you know he's lying?"

"He only had two other men on the ship, which means all the rest of his men are out somewhere else. My hunch is that they're monitoring every move the Reichswehr unit makes."

"Suppose you're right," Richard said. "Why would he lie to you when you're friends?"

"Does Kai ever need a reason to lie? It's just what he does. But if you want a legitimate reason, it's likely that he doesn't have enough men to watch the Germans and us. So he tried to get us to buy into his lie so we'd gallivant across the mainland in search of a seal that isn't there. Meanwhile, the Reichswehr unit could make off with it, and we'd have failed our mission."

"We should talk to someone else, maybe some other archeologists who could give us their estimation on where the seal is," Richard said. "At least, we should try to do this before we go anywhere."

Helen locked eyes with Richard. "I'm calling rank on this one. We're doing it my way. We'll leave for Macau first thing in the morning. We're going to follow the Reichswehr unit and hunt them down."

CHAPTER 6

D R. JEAN RENAULT'S BODY SLID DOWN AGAINST THE wall in the alleyway, his hands clutching his neck. In a matter of seconds, he fell limp and leaned over until his head hit the ground.

Reinhard knelt and wiped the blood from his blade on the archeologist's pants leg. After a few seconds, Reinhard checked for a pulse. Satisfied that he couldn't find one, he signaled for the two men standing in the shadows across the street to join him. The two soldiers raced over to Reinhard and took instructions on how to handle Renault's body.

Reinhard then turned toward Pierre Henry, Renault's diminutive assistant. "Your boss was a stubborn fool. We're glad you have more sense than him."

"Once you told me that he had stolen Dr. Miller's notes, how could I stay with him?" Henry said. "I don't want my name to be forever linked with such a disgrace."

"It won't be now," Reinhard said. "All you have to do is help us interpret these notes and affirm the story about Renault's death to the press and local authorities."

Henry sighed. "I don't mind playing my part if it means I will get credit for the discovery."

Reinhard smiled and patted Henry on the back. "You're going to have a long and prosperous career as an archeologist, especially with an approach to your profession like that."

"I'll do whatever it takes."

"That's what I like to hear," Reinhard said as he watched his two men scurry around on the ground and roll Renault's body up into a large blanket. "Now, let's get out of here before anyone sees us."

Reinhard and Henry cut down an alley, splitting away from the other Reichswehr soldiers. After five minutes of walking at a brisk pace, Reinhard glanced at Henry and then stopped to rest.

"How are you doing?" Reinhard asked.

Henry was bent over with his hands on his knees as he gasped for air. "I'll be fine. Just … give me … a minute."

"We need to keep moving," Reinhard said. "We don't want to give anyone here a reason to suspect us in your boss's death, especially you. If someone can place you near the last place anyone saw him alive, it's going to be trouble for you."

Henry's eyes widened. "You think someone saw us?"

"No, but you can never be too sure. I'd hate for you to lose your big opportunity at glory over an escape place that wasn't too tidy."

Henry stood upright and took a deep breath. "I'm ready to go."

Reinhard spun around and kept walking, returning to the main street. He noticed a couple of men stagger out of a bar and turn toward him.

"Keep your head down," Reinhard said through clenched teeth.

Henry complied with Reinhard's command, jamming his hands into his pocket and shuffling along behind Reinhard.

"Hey, little fellow," one of the men called. "Have you lost your mum? It's a little late for you to be out on the streets, isn't it?"

Reinhard glanced at Henry, who formed a fist with his hand. "Just ignore them, Henry. It's not worth it."

Henry turned around and glared at the men.

"Oh, so you want a fight, do you?" the man shouted at Henry. "Come back here and fight like the boy that you are. It won't take long for me to put you out."

Henry darted toward the men, but Reinhard snatched Henry by his collar and jerked him backward.

"What are you doing?" Henry asked. "That man needs what's coming to him."

"Yes, but you don't need what's coming to you if you provoke him," Reinhard said, steering Henry away from the crowd. "Let's just keep walking. We don't need any trouble."

"That's right," the man yelled. "Run away with your father. Go hide behind someone bigger than you."

Henry stopped and spun back toward the troublemakers. Before he could get more than a couple of feet away, Reinhard reached back and snatched Henry again.

"They will get what's coming to them from someone else," Reinhard said.

"Pierre?" another man called.

Reinhard nudged Henry forward and shielded him from seeing who the mystery person was. "If they identify you, your freedom and life will be in danger."

"I think I know who that is," Henry said.

"It doesn't matter."

"Yes, it does, if that's who I think it is. It's Edward Danforth, who is an archeological mercenary of sorts."

"I don't care if that was your father, you're not looking back," Reinhard said.

"If he's here, that means someone else is hunting for the seal."

"It just means that another archeological team is here.

This part of the world is teeming with artifacts."

Henry shook his head. "He only works for people who pay well, which means he's here hunting something big. I doubt he'd be here for a simple artifact. I'm sure he's here for the seal."

"Keep walking," Reinhard said. "We don't want him even to get the faintest idea that you are who he thinks you are."

Henry relented and kept walking with Reinhard before the two men darted down the next side street beyond earshot of the man Henry believed to be Danforth.

A couple of minutes later, a car pulled up next to them with one of the Reichswehr soldiers driving. The man motioned for them to get inside the vehicle. Without hesitating, both men dashed over to the waiting car and got inside.

"Where are we going now?" Henry asked.

"To get some rest," Reinhard said. "We've got a big day ahead of us tomorrow."

Henry leaned back in his seat and closed his eyes, leaving Reinhard alone with his thoughts. After a few minutes of silence, the driver held up an envelope.

"Sir, this came for you today," he said. "I thought you might want to read it."

Reinhard immediately recognized the handwriting. It was a letter from his wife Annemarie, obviously written before she died. He wanted to open it, but he couldn't bring himself to do it. She was gone, but as long as it remained unopened, Reinhard felt like she was still with him, that she still had something to say. He tucked the letter into his coat pocket and tipped his cap over his face before drifting off to sleep.

* * *

THE NEXT MORNING, WILHELM sat comfortably in his hotel room with a cup of coffee and perused a copy of an English newspaper from Hong Kong. The report on a recent storm and the sinking of a cruise ship interested him for a moment. But that was short-lived as a blaring headline arrested his attention: "Chinese Officials Divided over Artifacts." The article detailed a conflict brewing among several members of the Chinese government over the handling of the country's artifacts discovered by foreign archeologists. Wilhelm finally looked up when he noticed Reinhard shuffle into the room and stretch.

"Did you sleep well?" Wilhelm asked.

Reinhard shrugged. "I don't remember much after we were picked up, so I guess so."

"Well, you need to get ready because we need to move," Wilhelm said. "Henry already briefed me that he's certain another team is here looking for the seal as well."

"But they don't have Dr. Miller's notebook."

Wilhelm tapped the diary sitting on the end table next to him. "No, they don't. But if they figure out we're here, the situation could get messy. I want to get in and out of here as quickly as possible without attracting that much attention."

"If we unearth the seal, we're going to need people to know we found it so that our potential buyers believe it's authentic."

Wilhelm nodded. "Yes, but I don't want anyone snooping around our dig site. Speaking of which, the majority of our men, along with Henry, have already begun the preparations necessary to start digging. So hurry up and get dressed."

* * *

AN HOUR LATER, Wilhelm and Reinhard drove out to the dig site and strolled through the workers scurrying around the area. Some men had already begun carefully removing dirt and handing it over to another group that was sifting through it in search of any artifacts.

"Anything yet?" Wilhelm asked as he peered over one man's shoulder.

The man shook his head but didn't look up as he continued with his task.

"General Wilhelm, Commander Reinhard," Henry said as he approached the two Reichswehr leaders. "I need you to meet one of the local officials who oversees all archeological sites. I've tried to assure him that we will handle everything we find with the utmost care, but he needs your reassurances that this will happen."

"Of course," Wilhelm said. "I'll be more than happy to speak with him."

Henry led them over to the Chinese official, Xu Ling, who peered over the top of his glasses at the two Reichswehr officers.

"Are you in charge of this operation?" Ling asked.

Wilhelm nodded and offered his hand. "Yes, my name is Dr. Gerard from the University of Paris," he said in his best French-English accent.

"You need to end this excavation project right now," Ling said.

Wilhelm furrowed his brow. "What on earth for?"

"You didn't secure the proper paperwork."

"I most certainly did. I have it right here." Wilhelm fumbled around in his briefcase for a moment before removing a document he'd received just a day earlier.

"That is an application, not permission, Dr. Gerard," Ling said.

"That's not what I was told."

"Perhaps you need to listen more closely."

Wilhelm decided not to contest the claim any longer. "I apologize, Mr. Ling. I thought we had everything in order. And for the inconvenience, I'm truly and deeply sorry. Perhaps I can make it up to you some other way."

"Make it up to me?" Ling said. "I just want you to wait for approval before digging. There are many sites in the area that need to be preserved, and this is one of them. I don't know who even told you that it'd be possible to dig here."

"I was simply doing my best to abide by the rules and follow the directions we were given. This all comes as much of a surprise to me as it does to you. I've been doing this a long time, and I would never flaunt any government's ordinances regarding archeological dig sites."

Ling eyed Wilhelm's briefcase intently. "I appreciate the sentiment, but that doesn't change the fact that you must stop right this instance until you are cleared to begin again—if you're approved."

"Now, now, Mr. Ling. Let's not be too hasty. I'm sure we can work this out." Wilhelm dug into his briefcase and felt around for a stack of cash, which he proceeded to pull out.

"What's the meaning of this?" Ling asked as he eyed the money.

"As I was saying, Mr. Ling, I think we can work something out."

"If you intend to bribe me in some manner, I suggest you return your money and simply choose to abide by our protocol here."

Wilhelm gasped and stared wide-eyed at Ling. "I wouldn't dare think of such a thing. I just noticed that there is an additional fee once the permit has been approved. I thought I would give that to you now in an effort to expedite the process."

Wilhelm tried to hand Ling more than double the amount required.

Ling scowled and didn't touch it. "Payment is accepted once your permit is approved."

"We're in a bit of a hurry. I don't think there's any harm in taking this right now, is there?"

Ling looked over the top of his glasses at the money in Wilhelm's hand and shrugged. "Perhaps not, but I must warn you that if you are caught working on this site without the proper papers, you will be subject to a steep penalty and immediate rejection of your request. Is that understood?"

Wilhelm nodded and winked. "Of course, Mr. Ling. Now I'm sure you have much more important things to do than watching over us until the documents arrive. So, you can be on your way now. I'll make sure that these men comply with your demands."

"Very well then," Ling said before he spun and walked away. "I'll be back to check on you in the morning."

Wilhelm watched Ling exit the site before turning to Reinhard. "Everyone has their soft spot, don't they?"

Reinhard nodded. "I'm still wary of what's going to happen. Mr. Ling might also see an opportunity to bilk us for more money."

"Then we'll have to employ other methods to win him over."

Wilhelm stooped over and peered at what one of the men had uncovered.

"It's nothing, sir. Just an old piece of pottery," the man said.

"Keep up the good work."

When Wilhelm stood upright, he turned and found a young lad with an outstretched arm.

"A telegram for you, sir," the boy said.

Wilhelm took the note and tousled the boy's hair. "Thank you. Run along now."

"Who is it from?" Reinhard asked.

Wilhelm hadn't even unfolded the paper. "If it's for you, I'll let you know."

Once the telegram was fully opened, Wilhelm began reading it, his eyes widening as he did.

"What is it?" Reinhard asked.

"It's from General Seeckt. He wants us to return to Berlin at once. Apparently, he believes someone else can do the job better than we can."

Reinhard shrugged. "Perhaps he's right. We don't exactly have much to show for all our efforts."

"But we've got something from India—and once we get the heirloom seal, that will all change. We're not going anywhere."

CHAPTER 7

THE VOYAGE FROM HONG KONG TO MACAU WAS relatively smooth, especially considering how eventful Richard's previous trips had been. He spent most of his time sharpening his skills playing fan tan, a popular game at gambling houses all over Macau. Helen was more interested in talking with the ship's crew to see if they could tell her anything about the Germans, which was a fruitless venture.

Richard was seated at a table studying his cards when Helen pulled up a chair next to him. He placed a card on top of the pile and waited for the next one to appear so he could offload more of his hand.

"This is a pointless game," Helen said.

"No more pointless than searching in the wrong place," Richard quipped.

"You don't know it's the wrong place until you look there."

"Or unless someone tells you it is," he said as he slapped several more cards on the pile.

A couple of the players at the table shushed Richard and Helen.

"I appreciate how trusting you are of others," Helen said, lowering her voice to a whisper. "But that does us no good in this case. We need to leave no stone unturned."

"And lose days, maybe even weeks in our pursuit," Richard said as he tossed another card on the pile.

The player to his left dropped his final card on the stack in the center of the table and declared victory. He raked in the pot and flashed a smug grin at Richard.

"Speaking of losing," Helen said, "I told you this was a pointless game."

Richard sighed as he watched the dealer shuffle the cards. He stood as he eased out of his chair.

"Are you out?" the dealer asked.

Richard nodded. "Thanks for the games."

Helen followed him out onto the main deck. "I know you didn't agree with my suggestion to go to Macau."

"Suggestion?" Richard asked as his eyebrows shot upward. "I never once thought this was optional."

"Look, I know you believed Kai, but he's my friend, and I think you should trust my judgment in this one instead of being such a spoilsport. When we catch up with the Reichswehr, we need to be united."

"It's not that I don't trust you. I do. It's just that I have a hunch."

"Then trust my hunch that Kai is lying."

"Fine," Richard said. "But be prepared for a big 'I told you so' if the seal isn't there."

"If you say that to me, rest assured that I will punch you."

"It'd be one punch I'd gladly take."

"And one that'll never happen," Helen said with a wink. "The Germans know where it is. Let's go get something to eat."

As they strolled along the deck, Richard held his arm out for Helen, who took it and held him close. Their charade as a married couple had worked as a perfect cover, barely drawing a stray stare from any other passengers.

At the front of the ship, Richard noticed a man and stopped before turning to look out over the water, jerking Helen with him.

"What is it?" she asked.

"Don't look now, but I've met that man standing all alone leaning on the railing."

"Where did you meet him?"

"I believe it was in France. He looks like one of the men I saw at Dr. Thurston Miller's house."

"Was he an archeologist?" Helen asked.

"I'm not sure. Aside from the staff, there were several people milling around Dr. Miller's house a few days after his death was announced."

Helen shot a glance over her shoulder. "He looks British to me, maybe even working in intelligence."

"Whoever he is, I don't think it's mere coincidence that he's headed to Macau."

"Well, before you jump to any conclusions, perhaps we should find out what he's doing here."

Richard scowled. "I'm not going to ask him outright. He could recognize me."

"There are other ways," Helen said. "Leave it to me. I'll meet you in the bar in five minutes."

Richard followed Helen's instructions and waited for her. When she sat down next to him at the bar a few minutes later, she wore a wide grin.

"What did you find out?" he asked.

"He's in cabin 234," she said. "I'll keep him occupied while you go rifle through his belongings and see what you can learn about the purpose of his presence on this ship. Can you handle that?"

"Just give me ten minutes," he said.

Helen slipped him a bobby pin. "You might need this for the lock."

Richard thanked her and made his way toward the stairwell. He hustled down the steps and found the mystery man's room. After a few attempts, Richard managed to open the door. He eased inside and began to scurry around the room in search of anything that would provide a clue for why the familiar man was headed to Macau.

Using a flashlight, Richard's cursory scan of the cabin provided no immediate evidence. Aside from a small suitcase stashed in the corner, the room was rather bare. He picked his way through the clothes stacked neatly, which was filled with nothing but clothes. Only a suit hung in the closet.

Frustrated by the sparse items to inspect, Richard returned to the piece of luggage and decided to look more closely. He tapped the hard casing on the outside, which sounded hollow. Running his fingers along the seams of the inner lining, he felt a screw. He peeled back the material around the edges, revealing several small nodules. One by one, Richard turned them, allowing him access to a compartment hidden inside.

"Gotcha!"

Richard retrieved a folder from inside and began to scan the contents. The papers were marked as top secret and appeared to originate from British intelligence. He had barely read the first three sentences when he heard footsteps in the hallway and noticed a shadow cast beneath the door by a pair of feet.

Richard scrambled to put everything back into place before darting into the closet. He pulled his gun out of his pocket and held it close to his chest.

The light clicked on as the man entered the room. Richard steadied his breathing and prayed he wouldn't get caught. As he watched the man through the slats in the closet for a few moments, Richard was certain the man didn't suspect anything.

But seconds later, the door flung open, and Richard was face to face with the man—and his gun.

CHAPTER 8

WILHELM STRETCHED AS HE PREPARED TO RETURN to his hotel for the evening. He glanced once more at the telegram from Seeckt, which irked Wilhelm. Based on the curt nature of the note, Wilhelm concluded that either the report of their collection of jewels in Jaipur hadn't reached the German Reichswehr leader or it wasn't enough to impress him. But before being sent on the special mission, Wilhelm explained that his limited background in archeology and the art of uncovering such priceless artifacts would require a sharp learning curve.

What Wilhelm never counted on was a meddling agent to thwart his plans. But eventually, the American spy would be eliminated—and in a way that wouldn't draw the attention of the international community policing the German military's every move.

Wilhelm picked up a lantern, using it to light his path as he exited his quarters. He meandered through several areas, which were still teeming with workers scratching away at the soil. Reinhard stood waiting on the opposite side of cordoned off space.

"The evening crew arrived a half-hour ago," Reinhard said.

"Have they found anything yet that would lead us to believe we're hunting in the right spot?" Wilhelm asked.

"That's a question for Dr. Henry."

Pierre Henry looked up from his work and navigated his way over to Wilhelm.

"What do you want to know?" Henry asked.

"Was Dr. Miller onto something or was he off base in your estimation?" Wilhelm asked.

Henry shrugged. "It's hard to tell at this point. Dating the pieces we've found takes time, but my cursory look at the few parts we've collected says that Dr. Miller was brilliant and knew something nobody else did."

As Henry spun to return to his worksite, one of the men shouted excitedly as he rushed over to the French archeologist.

"What is it?" Henry asked.

Wilhelm and Reinhard shuffled next to them to see what the commotion was all about.

"Is that it?" Wilhelm asked.

Henry dusted off the piece of jade and examined it more closely. "Well, I can't be sure yet, but this looks just like the artifact Dr. Miller described in notes."

Handing the stone to Wilhelm, Henry dug into his pocket and pulled out Dr. Miller's notebook. He flipped through the pages until he reached a spot and stopped. With a wide grin, Henry opened the paper wide and turned it around so everyone could see.

Slack-jawed, Wilhelm stared at the sketch and then glanced back at the seal in his hand. They both resembled each other.

"This is it," Wilhelm said, hoisting it high above his head. "Seeckt is going to wish he ever sent that telegram."

The workers clapped and cheered as they jumped to their feet.

"Pay them," Wilhelm ordered Reinhard. "And buy this

man whatever he wants for dinner tonight. We found what we came for."

Wilhelm retreated to his quarters and placed the stone in a small locked box before tucking it away in his satchel. Then he sat down and continued on his report. He was still detailing the events when Reinhard entered the room.

"Everything is taken care of," he said. "Our men are packing up now."

Wilhelm smiled as he looked up. "Can you believe it, Hans? We found the heirloom seal, an item that has been lost for nearly a thousand years. Do you know what this is going to fetch?"

"It might be just enough to launch the Reichswehr back to military prominence, all outside the prying eyes of the allies."

"Exactly," Wilhelm said. "However, we need to get out of here as soon as possible. If word leaks out too soon that we found the seal, we're going to have a difficult time getting this back to Berlin."

"The next ship leaves Macau tomorrow evening at five o'clock."

"Make sure the entire unit has tickets and let's get home."

Reinhard smiled. "That's even better news than finding the seal."

Wilhelm nodded. "I thought you might like to hear that. And, Hans, I appreciate all that you've done for me during these past few missions. I know you're going back to a difficult situation with Annemarie gone. Just know that your sacrifice hasn't gone unnoticed and will be justly rewarded."

"Thank you, sir," Reinhard said as he exited the room.

Wilhelm collected all his papers and stuffed them into his briefcase before leaving his temporary quarters for the last time. Several members of his team rushed in and began packing up everything.

Wilhelm strode outside wearing an ear-to-ear grin. He was too lost in thought about his triumphant success that he didn't notice the boy crouching in the shadows.

CHAPTER 9

RICHARD SWALOWED HARD AS HE GLANCED AT THE man's gun barrel. After being exposed, Richard hoped he could talk his way out of the situation, even though he was unsure which direction he needed to go with a hastily devised explanation.

"I want some answers right now, or I start firing," the man said in a thick British accent.

"I'm holding a gun, too," Richard said.

"I see that—but if you so much as twitch, I'm pumping you full of so many bullets that you won't have a chance to return fire."

The man gestured with his gun for Richard to exit the closet, and he readily complied.

"What do you want to know?" Richard asked as he held up his hands in a posture of surrender. The man snatched the weapon from Richard's hand.

The man eyed Richard closely. "Let's start with the fact that you're hiding in my closet and presumably snooping through my stuff."

"I had a little too much to drink and somehow ended up in this cabin. By the time I realized it, I heard you coming and decided to hide."

"And then you drew your gun when I opened the closet door? Sorry, chap, but I'm not that gullible. You lie to me again, and I'm going to fire at your knee caps now and ask questions later."

"Okay, okay," Richard said. "I thought you were a spy, and you were following us."

"Us? Is there someone else inside that closet?"

"No, no. My wife is—"

"I told you not to lie to me again," the man said. "Perhaps you want to rephrase that last statement before I start shooting because I can tell you're not married."

Richard sighed. "You're right. What I meant was my colleague and I are a little apprehensive about our mission, and we thought you might be after us."

The man chuckled. "And that's clearly not the case is it?"

Richard shrugged. "It wouldn't seem that way, but you could be acting as if you didn't know who I was yet actually—"

The man laughed and held up his hand. "Enough with your hypotheticals. You're reaching so far, you might pull a muscle. I have no idea who you are, which gives me more incentive to shoot you and toss you overboard when no one is looking."

"That wouldn't be a very good idea because someone would most definitely come looking for me."

"Out here? In this part of the world?" the man said as his voice ascended an octave along with his eyebrows. "Perhaps I should ransom you instead."

"That'd be an even bigger mistake."

The man chuckled again. "You'll say anything to stay alive."

"Look, I saw your papers," Richard said.

"You're proving my point," the man said, still grinning.

"No, I'm telling you the truth. I saw those documents inside your suitcase, and it appears as though we're both chasing the same group of people, though I'm not sure what British intelligence's objective is in pursuing the Reichswehr. But it's evident to me that we're actually on the same side in this fight."

The man stared at Richard before easing into a chair positioned against the far wall.

"Now you believe me, don't you?" Richard asked.

The man nodded slowly. "Who are you again?"

"Why don't you tell me who you are first?"

"Niles Coleman, British intelligence," he said, offering his hand and dropping his gun for the first time during their conversation. "And you are?"

"Richard Halliburton, U.S. Army Intelligence."

"It's a pleasure to meet you, Mr. Halliburton. Based off all your assumptions, it appears as though you're correct— we are chasing the same group of miscreants."

"You'd only call them that if you haven't interacted with them yet. I can assure you that they deserve a far harsher nickname than that."

"What did they do to you?"

"They sent an assassin after me, who met an early demise."

"Only one?"

Richard nodded. "Only one that I know of, but that's part of the reason I'm a little nervous when I see someone milling about who stands out to me. I'm sure there will be more."

"Perhaps we can work together," Coleman said. "From the way you've described these Reichswehr soldiers, combining our efforts might be a wiser approach."

"I couldn't agree more," Richard said. "Now, what do you know about this particular mission?"

"Someone tipped us off that Dr. Thurston Miller's

notebook regarding an ancient Chinese seal was stolen from his holiday home in France," Coleman said. "He was a fellow professor who was worried that a group of Germans who came to Dr. Miller's house was pursuing the artifact for monetary reasons. When pressed further, the professor described one of the men there, and he matches the description of Hans Reinhard, who is one of the leaders of a secret Reichswehr unit we've been tracking."

"I didn't know who Reinhard at the time, but I saw several Germans there that I later encountered in Egypt."

"Were you the one responsible for stopping them in the Valley of the Kings?" Coleman said with a hint of admiration in his voice.

"I had some help, but I was there."

"Perhaps you need to be leading this mission since you are more familiar with these men than I am."

Richard shook his head. "No, you know more than we do about this particular mission. We're simply trying to track them."

"Let's not make things too complicated then. When we get to Macau, you and your colleague can ask around in the city if anyone has seen the Germans and knows where they're staying. I'll scout out the supposed location of their dig. Fair enough?"

"Sounds like a plan to me."

CHAPTER 10

TWO HOURS LATER, RICHARD AND HELEN PREPARED to exit the boat along with their new partner, Niles Coleman. Richard brought Helen up to speed on the plan, something she was less than thrilled about. However, she agreed to go along with them despite expressing her reservations.

"There's nothing to worry about," Richard said as he toted their luggage while walking down the ramp. "You met Niles. He understands the game."

"This isn't a game, Richard. We've been tasked with preventing the Reichswehr from amassing a fortune. You must understand that this isn't some adventure for you to write about in a book."

"I'm fully aware of what we're doing here, but I can be serious about this business while at the same time enjoying the mission. It's a special talent that I have."

She rolled her eyes and sighed. "Let's just hope your friend is who he says he is."

"If he wasn't, I doubt I'd be standing here right now."

Once they reached the dock, Richard and Helen were met by a throng of locals offering their services. Richard stumbled forward as he absorbed a bump from another man. Giving him a sharp glance, Richard relaxed when he realized it was Niles.

"Check your pocket later," Niles said before vanishing amidst the sea of people.

Richard and Helen resisted the relentless barrage of propositions to be guided around the city. Instead, Richard asked an elderly man seated on a park bench about the quickest route to downtown. He nodded north up the street they were on and smiled. Richard thanked him by depressing a shilling into the man's hand before strolling toward the city center with Helen.

After a short walk, they reached the downtown area that was teeming with gambling houses. It was nearly midnight, but the city was still full of life. Outside each one, women fanned themselves and smiled coyly at visitors while coaxing them inside. Some of the establishments offered free drinks, while others gave players a handful of chips to get started.

"Let's get settled before we start asking around," Helen said.

Richard agreed and they quickly found a suitable hotel. Using his negotiating skills, Richard managed to land the suite on the top floor for a regular room price. Once they placed their luggage in the room, Richard read the note from Niles.

"What does it say?" Helen asked.

"Niles says that he'll be staying at the Macau Grand Hotel tonight and to meet him there for tea tomorrow at 4 o'clock. He's checking in under the name of Will Umberton."

"So what do we do in the meantime?"

"I suggest we get some rest," Richard said. "We have a big day ahead of us tomorrow."

"I won't argue with that."

Richard scanned the room, gazing longingly at the plush canopy bed. After a few seconds, he sighed.

"What is it?" Helen asked.

"Nothing," he said. "I'll sleep on the couch in the parlor."

* * *

THE NEXT MORNING, Richard awoke when Helen shook him. He squinted at the sunlight streaming into the room through the windows she had thrown open. She was whistling a cheery tune.

"It's time to get up," she said.

Richard moaned as he flopped onto the floor with his blanket. "Do you have to be so happy about it?"

"We need to get moving if we're going to track down the Reichswehr soldiers in the area. Who knows when they might be leaving next? We don't have any time to waste."

Richard stumbled into the bathroom and tried to make himself presentable. After fifteen minutes, he joined Helen in the parlor.

"Ready for breakfast?" she asked.

He nodded and shuffled after her out of the room and down the hall. They descended the three flights of stairs and entered the hotel's dining hall. After a brief breakfast, they decided to fan out and scour the fantan houses in search of the Germans.

While Richard had only recently learned the game, he found it to be one that made fast friends of everyone at the table, no matter who was winning. In his estimation, fan tan was eighty percent chance, fifteen percent quick reflexes, and five percent strategy. He and Helen agreed to split up to cover more ground with a plan of reconvening around lunchtime.

Richard entered one of the houses and stopped at the door. "I need to find some information about people who may have been in Macau recently," Richard asked as he exchanged money for chips with the man behind a counter.

The man had a smoldering cigar stuffed in his mouth. He looked around and nodded in the direction of a portly gentleman clad in a white suit and seated alone at a booth.

Two men, presumably the knowledgeable man's bodyguards, flanked the sides of the table.

"That's Mr. Xu," the cashier said. "If anyone knows about visitors in Macau, he does."

"Thank you," Richard said as he slipped the man a coin and then scooped up all the chips.

Richard sauntered over to the man, who seemed engrossed in a ledger book. As Richard neared the white-suited gentleman, one of the bodyguards stepped forward, preventing Richard from taking another step.

"Pardon me," he said, peering around the side of the guard, "Mr. Xu, do you have a moment?"

Xu didn't look up, mumbling to himself as he flipped through the pages in his book.

"It'll only take a minute of your time," Richard persisted.

"Spend a few hours at my casino and then we'll talk," Xu said, still refusing to acknowledge his casino guest.

Richard realized he wasn't getting anywhere unless he complied with Xu's wishes. So with twenty dollars worth of chips, Richard found a seat at one of the tables and began playing. The hours ticked by quickly as his fortunes started to improve following a poor opening streak. By lunchtime, he had doubled what he initially brought and wasn't inclined to stop. However, a tap on his shoulder in between hands changed all that.

Richard turned around to see one of the bodyguards looming behind him.

"Mr. Xu will see you now," the man bellowed.

"Guess that means I'm out," Richard said as he stood up. That statement was followed by disappointed groans from the fellow players who'd grown fond of him over the course of the morning.

Richard followed the man across the room. Then he gestured for Richard to sit down at Xu's table.

"This is quite the establishment you have here," Richard said. "These fan tan houses must be quite profitable."

"Did you come here to talk business or did you have another question for me?" Xu said, his eyes scanning Richard.

Richard shifted in his seat as he glanced at the nearby guards. "Actually, I was wondering if you'd seen a contingent of Germans recently."

"People from all over the world visit my place. I'm afraid you'll have to be more specific."

"About a dozen men, most of them are of the strapping young men, while a pair of older men lead them. Have you seen them here in the past week?"

Xu stroked his chin and gazed off in the distance. "What is it that you want with these men?"

"We have some unfinished business," Richard said.

The man grinned cheekily. "That's my favorite kind. Right boys?" He shot a quick look at the two guards, who nodded and smiled.

"So, have you seen them?" Richard pressed.

"I believe so. They came in a day ago or so. I'm not sure where they're staying, but you can check the hotels in the area. Someone will know. But I don't think they're here to gamble. They appear to have some other purpose."

"Thank you, Mr. Xu. You've been most helpful."

Xu shrugged and returned his attention to his ledger.

Richard checked his watch and hustled back to the hotel where Helen was waiting for him.

"Any luck?" he asked.

She shook her head. "I think everyone here is too busy gambling and playing fan-tan even to notice what color shirt their neighbor is wearing. What about you?"

"I spoke to the man who ran the fan tan house I visited, and he said the Germans are here but didn't offer up much information beyond that."

As they were talking, Niles approached their table.

"Niles?" Richard asked with a furrowed brow. "You're here. How did you find us?"

"They found it," Niles said.

"The seal?" Helen asked.

Niles nodded. "We need to get tickets for the Sui An, which departs the dock at five o'clock this evening."

"Where did you learn about this?" Richard asked.

"I went out to the dig site and talked with one of the locals who was working with them. I paid him twice what he was paid by the Germans."

"Good work," Helen said. "Richard and I will secure tickets then we need to meet back in an hour to discuss how we're going to retrieve the stone."

"Taking it back while at sea is risky, but it might be effective," Niles said. "The man I spoke with told me the leader—who I presume to be Karl Wilhelm—placed the stone in a lockbox."

"We'll figure out something," Richard said.

* * *

RICHARD LUGGED THEIR BAGS up the ramp as he and Helen boarded the Sui An, a steamship that would make the five-hour voyage back to Hong Kong. They settled into their cabin and waited for Niles to join them.

A half-hour later as the ship was shoving off from port, a knock at the door sent Helen scurrying over to see who was there. She opened it a crack and noticed Niles before ushering him inside.

"Did you see any members of the Reichswehr unit?" she asked.

"They're all aboard," Niles said. "I already spotted several of them at the fan tan tables."

"And what about Wilhelm?" Richard asked. "Where was he?"

"I saw him in the lounge getting drinks with one of his men."

Richard nodded. "That's probably Hans Reinhard. We need to separate them if we're going to have a chance to steal the seal from Wilhelm. And it's going to have to be someone other than me to do it since they will recognize me."

"Can you distract them?" Niles asked. "Perhaps you could draw Reinhard away and then we could make the switch."

"A switch?" Helen asked.

"Yes," Niles said as he produced a jade stone from his pocket. "I found a replica souvenir while I was downtown. It's supposedly the same size as the famed heirloom seal."

Helen cocked her head to one side. "But your informant told you it was in a lockbox."

"I found a small one in the market," Niles said. "I'm counting on this to work."

"We all are," Richard said. "And it's going to. But I suggest we wait until we get closer to port so we don't give Wilhelm much time to discover that he's been hoodwinked by us."

"Agreed," Helen said.

Niles rummaged around in his bag. "I also got you something," he said to Richard.

"What on earth?" Richard said as he gawked at the hat Niles displayed.

"To help you keep a low profile," Niles said. "I don't expect you're going to stay cooped up in your cabin during this trip and thought you might appreciate something to help you move about incognito."

"Thank you," Richard said as he situated the hat on his head.

Helen adjusted the bill so that it cast more shade over his eyes. "Put on a pair of these glasses, and nobody will know it's you."

"Of course they won't," Richard said. "You're hiding my entire face."

"No," Helen countered, "I'm simply making you look smart."

Richard watched his colleagues share a laugh at his expense. "You two fancy yourselves as comedians, don't you?"

"That's my next occupation if this spy gig doesn't pan out," Niles said.

Richard shook his head and huffed a soft laugh through his nose. "I'll be in my room if you need me."

Richard trudged down the hallway along with Helen before the sound of gunshots arrested their attention. Shouting and screaming commenced along with a chaotic stampede. Richard plastered himself against the wall and looked at Helen.

"Can you understand what they're saying?" he asked.

"Something about pirates," Helen said, stopping next to Richard.

"Pirates?" Richard said, his eyes twinkling.

Helen subtly shook her head. "No, this is not something to get excited about. Our lives are probably in danger, but I can tell what you're thinking."

"There's nothing wrong with looking forward to witnessing a siege by a group of pirates."

"What do you think is going to happen? Long John Silver is going to come thumping down the hall on his peg leg while the parrot perched on his shoulder repeats his commands?"

Richard pointed at Helen and smiled wryly. "Your imagination is more vivid than mine. I hadn't yet thought of all the details and—"

"Snap out of it," Helen said. "These pirates are dangerous, and they just might gut us with their swords. That'll be after they pillage our pockets for every valuable thing we have."

About that time, a man stormed around the corner and began barking at people and waving both his gun and a dagger around in the air.

"What's he saying?" Richard asked.

"Everyone has to go to the ballroom immediately," she said. "Anyone who doesn't will be shot if discovered."

"Should we make a break for it?" Richard asked. "I think we're still close enough to the shore that some fishing vessel would find us before we got too tired of treading water."

"Are you mad?" Helen asked. "Our mission is still intact no matter what's going on here. We can't let the Reichswehr escape with the seal."

"It's not the Reichswehr that I'm worried about right now," Richard said with a shrug. "Besides, the pirates are just going to take it from the Germans anyway."

The unruly scene transformed into a subdued one as the pirates methodically herded all the passengers into the ballroom and rifled through their personal belongings. Some of the discoveries at the bottom of the ladies' purses resulted in several breath-taking moments. But for the most part, the thieving was rote. The pirates plunged their hands into pockets and other bags in search of something. Throughout the process, the hulking pirate conducting the searches with the help of his minions amassed a small fortune, stuffing jewelry, watches, and money into a large sack. However, a hush fell over the room as a woman wielding a sword in one hand and a gun in the other pushed her way to the center of the room. She fired a shot in the air to announce her presence.

"I am Captain Yang," she said in English. "We are not here to hurt you, but we are looking for a specific item. It's an ancient Chinese artifact that looks like this."

She gestured toward one of her men, who held up a jade-colored stone about the size of a small pinecone.

"If you know that one of your fellow passengers has this stone, please let one of my men know," she continued. "It will be much easier on everyone."

She scanned the room, spinning around in search of anyone who might volunteer the information.

Richard watched her closely for a moment before searching the sea of faces for the Reichswehr unit. After a few moments, he identified Wilhelm and Reinhard, who were standing about ten meters apart against the far wall.

"All right," she said. "Your silence has spoken volumes. We'll go through every single item you possess on this ship until we find it. And this process begins right now."

The pirates split into groups of three and began combing through the belongings of each passenger. Eight teams fanned out among the people and commenced the humiliating procedure. Richard didn't take his eyes off Wilhelm.

"We need to do something," Helen said.

"What do you suggest?" Richard asked.

"I don't know. You're always the one ready to act on a moment's notice before you even give much thought to your actions. I thought for sure you'd just be waiting for the right time to beat back these pirates."

Richard smiled. "You're right on one count—I do have a plan."

He whistled and gestured for one of the nearby pirates to come to him.

"Want to end this right now?" Richard asked.

The man nodded. "You know who has the seal?"

Richard shrugged. "Maybe. I just need to speak to your captain first."

The pirate spun on the heels of his boots and scurried over to Yang. She stooped down to hear what the man was saying before standing upright and striding over to Richard.

"What do you want?" she asked.

"What do you want with the seal?" Richard fired back.

"It's none of your business," she said.

"Then perhaps it's none of my business to tell you who has it."

She smirked. "We'll find it one way or another. And when we do, I'm going to treat you as if you were the person who refused to give it to me."

"You'd be making a terrible mistake," Richard said. "Now, I'm not inclined to tell you the identity of the person hiding the seal, but if you promise to leave the boat immediately and not hurt another soul, I'll tell you."

"Look, Wang," she said with a soft chuckle, "we have our knight who wants to save everyone. Well, that's not how my men operate. We don't make concessions for any reason."

Richard shrugged. "By the time you get to this person, who knows where the object might be. Certainly by that time, the authorities will be looking for the Sui An once they realize it's still out at sea. And then you'll be in a far more difficult situation. But you're smart. I trust you'll make the right decision."

She glanced at her watch. "Fine," she said with a snarl, "tell me who it is."

Richard averted making eye contact with Wilhelm but

nodded in his direction. "See the tall man against the wall wearing the gray blazer and red tie?"

Yang nodded.

"That's your man," Richard said after he did little more than glance in Wilhelm's direction.

She eyed Richard up and down. "You better not be trying to make a fool out of me."

"I'd never do that in a situation like this," Richard said.

Across the room, Wilhelm shifted nervously from one foot back to the other as he stared at the ground. Richard managed to avert a steely glare from the German, who hadn't yet recognized the man who'd squealed.

Captain Yang gestured for one of her teams to head directly toward the back of the room and retrieve Wilhelm. Once he was positioned in the center of the room, she stripped him down and rummaged through all his clothes until she found the seal.

She held it up high above her head triumphantly as she discreetly pocketed Wilhelm's knife and gun. "This is what we came for, and thanks the cooperation from one of your passengers who notified us who was concealing the stone, we're going to leave you in peace."

Yang snatched a pearl necklace off a woman who was standing nearby. She shrieked and then protested, which was met by a firm shove from Yang, knocking the woman to the ground.

As the pirates paraded through the ballroom, Richard's mouth fell agape as another steamer pulled up next to the Sui An and ushered aboard the pirates, who utilized the ship's lifeboats in workmanlike fashion. Captain Yang was the last one to exit the ship, firing one final shot into the air before repelling down a rope to the raft waiting below. The pirates cheered as she descended, their shouts filling the night air while the passengers crowded the deck and watched their tormentors disappear into the darkness.

Helen eased up next to Richard. "I hope you're proud of yourself. When the Germans had the stone, we at least knew where they were—and where it was."

"But the Germans don't have the stone anymore," Richard said. "And wasn't that the goal of this mission?"

"If you think that Reichswehr unit is going to quietly return to Berlin after that, you don't know your enemy."

Richard smiled. "I fully expect them to pursue the seal—and we're going to make sure they never get it."

CHAPTER 11

W ILHELM RETERATED TO HIS ROOM WHILE THE Sui An limped back to the Hong Kong harbor. The pirates had severely damaged the steamer's engine just before departing as an insurance policy against being pursued across the water. Fortunately, the ship could still navigate and move, but only at a quarter of the speed, according to the announcement that came across the intercom system.

"I had it in my hands," Wilhelm said aloud as he paced around the room.

Reinhard reclined in a chair in the corner of the room and swirled the wine around in the glass he was holding. "That's becoming a common theme on our missions."

Wilhelm stopped and snarled at Reinhard. "And one I want to end immediately or else General Seeckt might replace us permanently. While I am fiercely committed to the nature of our assignment, I couldn't exactly blame him if he saw fit to make a change. We're not getting the job done."

"I'd suggest that we've stumbled into some unfortunate situations."

"That's not how Seeckt is going to see this. The bottom line is that we've done nothing but fail."

Reinhard shrugged. "At least the pirates should be easier to defeat than the American."

Wilhelm narrowed his eyes and clenched his jaw. "Don't

get me started on Richard Halliburton. I swear if I see him again, I'll rip his arms off with my bare hands."

"We can't worry ourselves with him anymore," Reinhard said. "We need to return home soon and have something in our hands for Wilhelm. We can't spend any more time bemoaning the past."

"No," Wilhelm said. "But killing that American spy could be helpful for our future endeavors."

Reinhard drained the rest of his drink and set the glass down on the desk. "Based on the captain's report, we're in for a slow ride back to Hong Kong. I suggest you get some rest and we'll sort everything out when we get to port."

Wilhelm grunted. "What's to sort out? We're going to get a boat and go after those pirates before that seal vanishes again or gets sold to some reputable museum."

"And how do you plan to secure a boat? We barely have enough money to cover food and transportation until we return home. What makes you think we'll have some vast treasure chest to dip into?"

"Those bastard allies," Wilhelm said as he resumed his pacing. "They've crippled the Reichswehr with their diplomatic overtures. Meanwhile, the German people pay the highest price because the one entity designed to protect them can't do its job on a shoestring budget."

Wilhelm looked at his fellow military leader, who opened his mouth as if he were going to say something but apparently decided against it.

"Look, I know what we're doing has an eye on the future, not on the present, but you can't deny how difficult it is for us to reacquire the money necessary to rebuild our country's military."

"That's precisely the point why they've hamstrung our operation," Reinhard said. "The allies fear us. They know what we're capable of doing. Only the next time we strike against them, we won't lose."

Wilhelm nodded briefly before his bobbing morphed into shaking his head. "Yet that still doesn't change anything for our situation. If we're going to ever regain our footing along with our respect in this world, we need to find a way to fill our coffers. The victors of war always have the deepest treasure chests and other advantages."

"Or a more sound strategy."

Wilhelm lifted his index finger and poked at the air above his head. "Which is how we're going to claim victory as it pertains to that hidden seal."

"So you have a new idea?" Reinhard asked.

"I'm forming one," Wilhelm said. "I just need to sleep on this idea for a few hours."

Reinhard kicked his shoes off and leaned back on his bed. "Wake me when your moment of genius strikes you."

Taking a cue from Reinhard, Wilhelm settled on his bed and closed his eyes. He knew what he had to do, but he wasn't sure he could get the kind of help necessary to pull it off.

* * *

THE HORN BELLOWED on the top deck, waking up a ship full of disoriented passengers. Wilhelm wasn't one of them, awake and focused on what he needed to do next. He decided to take a morning stroll to get an idea for when they might be arriving in port.

In a brief moment of levity, he chuckled at some of the people shuffling down the hallways and asking questions about the events that transpired the night before as if they weren't convinced the pirate takeover of the ship actually happened. He hadn't laughed in a while and hadn't even considered it a possibility since the seal had been ripped from his possession by a band of pirates. Someone who had worked on the dig team had obviously leaked the news, setting himself up as a target. He made a mental note to scrutinize any local help in the future.

As he rounded the corner, he was pleased to see the Sui An nearing the Hong Kong port. One of the ship's mates stopped next to him and took a deep breath of the fresh morning air.

"Looks like we made it," Wilhelm said to the man.

The man glanced at Wilhelm and sneered. "No thanks to you. We were in this predicament because of your greed."

Wilhelm seethed. "My greed? The pirates are the reason we are in this situation, not me. My personal cargo didn't cause this situation."

"You keep believing that. The world would be much better off if you Germans weren't around."

Wilhelm narrowed his eyes and contemplated flinging the man overboard before deciding against it. He walked away, biting his tongue and hoping for a future encounter with the man to set the record straight.

When Wilhelm returned to his room, Reinhard was already up and dressed.

"You were up early," he said.

Wilhelm nodded. "I know what we need to do to take the seal back from those thieves."

"Does it involve stealing a ship?"

Wilhelm grinned. "This is why you're my second in command. You know me too well."

"It's the only move we have if Seeckt isn't going to loosen the treasury and provide some financial assistance."

"Seeckt believes we're going to fail. We're going to prove him wrong. Go let the rest of the troops know that they need to be ready the moment we dock. We don't have a minute to waste."

* * *

LED BY WILHELM, the Reichswehr unit was first in line to leave the Sui An. The German soldiers flanked their commander and tried to act casually as they strode along the docks. Wilhelm took them to a business located away from the more commercial ships and inquired about borrowing a ship for a fee.

The bespectacled owner of the establishment laughed at Wilhelm's request. When Wilhelm didn't crack a smile, the man realized the German was serious.

"Allowing someone to take one of my ships out of port isn't what we do here," the man said.

"What if I compensated you handsomely for it? Would that be something you do then?" Wilhelm asked.

Reinhard nudged Wilhelm and spoke in a hushed tone. "Are you forgetting we don't have the money?"

Wilhelm nudged back and shot a knowing glance at Reinhard.

"I suppose if the price is right, I would be willing to consider it," the man said.

"What would be the right price for you?" Wilhelm asked.

"Hmmm," the owner said as he stared contemplatively beyond the German contingent and across the water. "That's a good question. How much do you have?"

"More than enough. Now name your price."

The man shrugged and then picked up a piece of paper and scribbled down a number on it. "Do you have this kind of money?"

Wilhelm's eyes widened. "I'm not made of gold, but I do have a substantial amount to offer you if the price is more reasonable."

With a sigh, the man crumpled up the paper and flung

it into the trash can nearby. "I guess we have nothing further to discuss."

Wilhelm raised his hands in the air and shook his head. "Now, now. Let's not be so hasty. This is a negotiation, right?"

The man wrinkled his nose. "If you think so."

"I need to know if I'm wasting my time with you or working in good faith. Right now, I'm desperate to get into a ship and sail to Macaw. However, if I had the kind of money you're suggesting, I'd be able to afford a boat far better than the one docked outside here."

"Tell you what," the man said before taking a deep breath, "I'll let you borrow the boat for one day for this price."

He scratched out another number and slid it across the counter for Wilhelm to read.

"Are you insane, man?" Wilhelm asked. "That's still a ridiculous amount."

"Take it or leave it. No one else around here is going to loan you their ship for anything less than that."

Wilhelm grunted. "In that case, I'll take it."

The man smiled, unaware of what Wilhelm's response meant. The German commander pulled out his gun and trained it on the shop owner. He threw his hands in the air and backed up a couple of steps before hitting the wall behind him.

"I don't want any trouble," the owner said.

"Of course you don't," Wilhelm said. "You just want to gouge me, pocketing all that cash at a ridiculous cost."

"That's not at all what I meant by naming that price," the man said. "I just want to charge you a fair amount, that's all. I have a tendency to undercharge customers. And at the end of the day, I have to face my brother, who is my business partner in this venture. And with all due respect, I'm more afraid of him than I am your weapon there."

A faint smile crept across Wilhelm's lips. "Let me relieve you of that burden then."

"No, no, no–"

A gunshot cracked through the air before the owner staggered backward and then slumped against the wall. He slid to the ground, leaving a stained wall behind him.

Wilhelm knelt down next to the man, who was clinging on for life. "I promise your brother won't care anymore about how you undercharge customers."

Moments later, the man fell limp.

"Let's get moving, gentlemen," Wilhelm said to his soldiers. "We've got a ship to sail."

CHAPTER 12

RICHARD PEERED OVER THE TOP OF THE CROWD shuffling toward the exit ramp of the Sui An and scanned the area for the Reichswehr soldiers. He squinted into the distance, unsure if he could trust his 22-year-old pair of eyes. A man behind Richard jostled into him, setting off a chain reaction that affected the next three people.

"Did you see anything?" Helen asked, ignoring the bumping and shoving from the throng of passengers anxious to leave the ship.

Richard shook his head. "Not anything I can be sure of. I thought I saw a large group near the end of the dock, but I can't be certain."

"That'll be a good place to start, I suppose," Helen said.

"As good as any since I don't have any idea where they went." He tapped his watch and cursed under his breath. "If only this thing hadn't stopped working early this morning. It felt later to me than my watch said, but when I saw that it was only six-thirty, I chalked up the difference to a rough night at sea."

"You're supposed to trust your gut, remember?"

Richard sighed. "My gut is hungry and the rest of me is irritated because of it. Don't trust anything out of my mouth until I get some food in my belly."

Helen stood on her tippy toes as they approached the ramp. As the passengers in front of them descended, they had an unobstructed view of the harbor for the first time.

"Look over there," she said, pointing at the end of the dock. "Is that who you saw?"

Richard nodded. "That's them all right."

"Let's hurry. We can't let them get too far." She elbowed her way through the crowd until she reached an impasse, a line six-men wide. The hulking men created a formidable wall, swallowing up every free inch between them with their massive muscles.

"Excuse me," she said as she tried to wedge her head through a pair of biceps belonging to two men. "I need to get through."

One of the men slowly glanced down at her. "Going somewhere?"

"I'm trying to," she said as she succeeded in jamming one of her arms between the two men. However, getting any farther proved to be a challenge she couldn't conquer. The two men grinned at each other as they applied pressure to Helen's arm, forcing her to shriek in pain.

"Gentlemen," Richard began, "I mean, you are gentlemen, right?"

The men who bothered to turn around sneered at Richard.

Richard clapped his hands. "OK, now that we have settled, can we get back to the business of releasing my lady friend here and allowing her to do her job?"

"And what job is that exactly?" one of the men said as he held his ground amidst the crush from the other passengers.

"She's a reporter and needs to file a story as soon as possible about the pirates attacking the Sui An last night,"

Richard said. "Surely you want those men apprehended for what they did to us all aboard this ship."

The man nodded as he moved aside, allowing Helen and Richard to pass. However, despite their efforts to navigate the maze of people, they remained woefully far from the front. When they finally made it to the dock, a representative from the ferry company presented them with a voucher for a future trip, a gesture that was met by most of the passengers with disgust.

"I'm sorry we couldn't stop them for you," Richard said, surprising the man with a brief moment of kindness.

"You have nothing to be sorry for. We should've been able to protect you from such a humiliating crime. And unfortunately, we couldn't make that happen. While we can't replace everything that was taken from you, we hope that you'll consider using our services again in the future."

Richard stuffed the voucher into his pocket and turned his attention to the end of the docks where he noticed a ship launching into the harbor.

"Do you see that?" Helen asked, pointing toward the ship.

Richard nodded. "We need to run."

They both broke into a sprint, sidestepping a few elderly women who were lugging their bags behind them. One of the ladies held up her cane and shook it at Richard.

"Watch where you're going," she yelled.

Richard spun around to face her while continuing to run backward along the deck. "Sorry, ma'am," he said, flashing a faint smile to accompany his genteel Tennessee charm.

Her frown vanished, replaced with a wide-eyed grin.

"We're after those pirates," he said before turning forward again and racing to catch up with Helen.

Once he finally did, she shot him a sideways glance. "Flirting with little old ladies? You ought to be ashamed of yourself."

"It's not flirting; it's being personable. There's a difference."

She flashed him a wry smile and shook her head as the pair continued to hustle toward the edge of the harbor where they'd seen the boat leave from. Richard estimated it would take at least ten minutes for them to reach that point as they ran through the sprawling Hong Kong harbor. And that was even before they had a chance to secure a seafaring vessel.

When they reached the location the ship had departed from, Richard noticed a commotion inside the small office nearby. He rushed over to it and asked what was happening. But before he received an answer, he noticed a man bleeding and being attended to be a doctor and a pair of young men.

"What happened here?" Richard asked.

A young boy standing nearby explained. "A group of Germans shot my uncle after he denied them usage to one of our boats."

Richard nodded as his eyes bounced between the lad and the man fighting for his life.

"Stand back," the doctor ordered, pushing away a man who was hovering too close to the injured fellow.

"But he's my brother," the man protested as he eased away.

Richard approached the man. "I'm so sorry about this."

The man narrowed his eyes and glared at Richard. "Who are you?"

"I'm actually chasing down those men," Richard said. "My partner and I are—"

"Your partner?" the man said as he cast a furtive glance at Helen. "You're with her?"

"Don't let her sweet appearance fool you. She could just as easily slam you to the ground as she could whip up a breakfast fit for a king. And you need to choose which side of her you'd like to see as these men have taken something that doesn't belong to them—and she's not really happy about it."

The man seethed. "I don't care how you do it, but I want them to pay for what they did to my brother."

"Do you have another ship?" Richard asked.

The man nodded. "It's not as fast as the one the Germans took, but we might still be able to overtake them with a competent crew."

"Do you have the right crew available?" Helen asked.

"Can you follow directions?" the man asked.

"Let's go," Richard said. "We don't have any time to lose."

The man introduced himself as Captain Chow Yen before ushering Richard and Helen to his ship, the Xian Dao. He signaled for two other boys to get onto the boat, explaining that they were his nephews, Lei and Shing, and could help with the navigation of the ship.

Minutes later, they were cruising through open waters. Richard stood at the bow and scanned the horizon through a pair of binoculars. After a long search, he identified the ship.

"I see it," he said. "It's heading due west."

"They're going to Lantau Island," Yen said.

"What's on Lantau?" Helen asked.

"Not much more than pirates and a few terrace farmers," Shing said, joining the conversation.

"That makes sense," Richard said. "We were on the Sui An yesterday that was attacked by a bunch of pirates who raided everyone on board."

"What did they take?" Yen asked.

Richard handed the binoculars to Helen. "They took the seal of the realm."

Lei's eyes widened. "The seal of the realm?"

"You know that is an ancient myth," Yen said. "It's a way to get tourists to buy souvenirs in the market."

Richard shrugged. "Maybe, but I saw it—and these pirates were willing to attack a ship to take it back."

"I don't believe it," Yen said.

"Whether you believe the legend or not, there is an ancient Chinese artifact that the Reichswehr is intent on taking to the black market and profiting off it as much as possible."

"Everyone in our entire nation has been searching for that stone for ages," Shing said. "They can't kill my uncle and take the seal."

"That's what they're going to do if we don't stop them," Richard said. "The leader of the pirates—"

"Captain Yang?" Yen asked.

Richard cocked his head to one side. "You know her?"

"She's a bit of a legend around these parts. At times, she presents herself as someone who cares about the poor. Other times, it's quite evident that she's only interested in making herself rich."

"We're not sure what her motives are this time, but we don't really care," Helen said.

"You don't care?" Lei asked. "That seal belongs in a museum, a place where everyone in China and Hong Kong can appreciate the significance of such an artifact."

"I agree," she said. "But none of that will matter if the Reichswehr sailing in your stolen vessel catches up with Captain Yang and her crew first. What we experienced on the Sui An wasn't a fair fight. However, I can promise you that if the Germans get to her before we do, the fight won't be all that fair either. No matter how skilled those pirates are, they will be eliminated one by one until the seal is found."

Richard took another peek through his binoculars at the horizon.

"What do you see?" Yen asked.

"They just vanished around the backside of Lantau Island."

"They know what they're doing," Yen said. "That's where the pirates' hideout, though it's a well-known secret. As long as they don't harass Hong Kong's own, the police don't much care."

"Would they care about this robbery on the high seas?" Helen asked.

"Probably not since they took the seal from a group of Germans. However, they're opening themselves up to attacks from other marauders interested in getting their hands on that priceless artifact."

"Oh, there's a price for that rock," Richard said. "Someone would pay a small fortune to keep it in their private collection. And that's exactly why the Germans went after it."

"How much farther?" Helen asked.

"Well, we're not going to catch them, if that's what you're asking," Yen said.

"Your crew wasn't competent enough?" she asked.

Yen chuckled. "They had too much of a head start. But the tides are low and they won't be able to get all the way to shore. You might be able to make up some time that way."

"What do you mean?" she asked.

Yen cast a sideways glance at Helen. "How fast can you row?"

Ten minutes later, the Xian Dao turned around the end

of Lantau Island as Yen set a course for a group of caves near a small cove. Richard realized what Yen was doing.

"We can't get up to the shore with the tide coming in like it is," Yen said. "I'm already pushing the boundaries of what's possible. You're going to have to get to the shore using one of our rafts."

Richard surveyed the water, which was choppy due to strong crosswinds. "How close can you take us?"

"Maybe another five hundred meters," Yen said.

Richard furrowed his brow. "That'll leave us with an hour of rowing before we reach the shore."

"You both appear to be in fine physical shape and shouldn't be a—"

Yen cut his response short as the ship jerked backward, coming to an abrupt halt. Richard eyed the captain carefully.

"Please tell me that's not what I think it is," Richard said.

Yen smiled sheepishly. "Sorry, but did I say five hundred meters? I meant one."

Helen stamped her foot. "We're stuck on a sandbar, aren't we?"

Yen pushed his way past both of them and hustled down the stairs leading to the main deck. Without a word, he ripped a tarp off one of the rafts and began to unwind the rope.

"Get in," he finally said.

Richard and Helen complied, jumping inside. Minutes later, they were straining at the oars, fighting against the water to reach the shore. Little more than grunts and groans were voiced between them. Richard took a peek toward the cove and saw two rafts beached near the entrance to the caves.

"You ready to take these Germans on?" Richard asked.

Helen set her jaw and glared at him, refusing to pause

from her rowing. "This is what I get for listening to you and your bright ideas."

"Look on the bright side," Richard said. "At least no one knows we're coming."

A few seconds later, he heard a gunshot ring out from the cave.

"Did you hear that?" Richard asked.

Helen nodded. "We better hurry or we're going to be an easy target."

A bullet whizzed past them, splashing down in the water nearby.

"Looks like we already are," he said as he saw a handful of pirates taking cover in the trees and firing at the raft.

CHAPTER 13

WILHELM SPLIT UP HIS TEAM AS THEY APPROACHED the pirates' cave. He led one group while Reinhard led the other. During the war, Wilhelm had fought in a wide variety of terrains, but this was new territory for him.

"Are you sure this is the right place?" Wilhelm asked Ludwig.

Ludwig dug a map out of his back pocket and showed the circled location to his commander. "According to what they told me, this is the right spot."

Wilhelm shrugged and crept forward along the beach toward the entrance. He watched as Reinhard's unit vanished into the thick forest just beyond the shoreline in search of another way in.

"This place looks deserted to me," one of the soldiers said. "Could this be someone's idea of a prank on us?"

Wilhelm shook his head. "I know this doesn't appear promising, but I think the people around here want these marauders gone, even if they are known for only robbing wealthy tourists. Just keep moving forward and be prepared for anything. I'm more inclined to think this could be an ambush than a joke."

Once they reached the mouth of the cave, Wilhelm checked over his shoulder one final time before entering. He scrambled over a series of rocks and small boulders in the darkness. After he reached the top of one boulder, he signaled for the rest of his troops to join him.

When everyone arrived, he turned and looked inside the cave, which had opened up into a vast cavern, lit overhead by sunlight streaming through a large hole fifty meters above them. The outer edged was ringed with a passageway that led to other tunnels. A small stream cut through the center, providing a fresh water source. On the ground, pirates scurried back and forth, toting an array of objects from clothes and food to guns and ammunition. He recognized a couple of them who had attacked them on the Sui An.

"This isn't a joke," Wilhelm said. "These are the same people who stole the seal from us, and we're going to take it back."

He instructed his troops to spread out along the interior ring of the cave and stay low until he gave them a signal. Crawling into position, Wilhelm steadied his gun against a rock and then raised his hand before bringing it down swiftly.

Gunfire echoed throughout the cave as several men dropped to the ground, clutching their new wounds. Wilhelm chuckled as he took aim at a man toting a basket laden with rice. The grain spilled out as the man crumpled to the ground. A bullet whizzed past Wilhelm's head, forcing him to retreat to a safer position.

For the next ten minutes, Wilhelm's unit fired on the pirates. Most of the ones who abandoned their items were able to escape unscathed to the opposite side of the cave. But the men who clung to their objects were slowed by the craggy floor and became easy targets. Other pirates emerged from the other side and returned fire. The standoff didn't do much more than burn through all the ammunition either side held. Once it was clear no more shots were being fired, the pirates armed with swords and daggers rushed the German invaders.

Wilhelm looked at Ludwig. "Go find the seal."

Ludwig crept off in the shadows, taking cover inside the makeshift corridor that encircled the cave's large opening.

"Prepare yourselves, wolfsrudel," Wilhelm said.

Wilhelm's men handled the first wave of attackers with ease. The Reichswehr's military training proved to be far more than the pirates could handle. Once they had killed their foes, Wilhelm did a quick health assessment and learned that only one of his men had suffered a slash across his bicep in combat.

He glanced across the cave at the next wave of men ready to assault his troops. "That's a good report, but we're going to have to keep this up, at least until Ludwig returns with the seal."

Instead of sending a-half dozen men to fight the Germans, the pirates doubled their fighters to outnumber the Reichswehr more than two to one. The fighting was more intense as Wilhelm fell backward and had a knife to his throat before one of his men bashed in the attacker's head with a rock. Wilhelm got up and dusted himself off, grateful to still be alive.

He peered out across the cave and saw Ludwig racing toward their position and clutching something in his hand.

Ludwig made eye contact with Wilhelm. "I got it."

But before he could reach the base of the incline leading up to Wilhelm, one of the pirates emerged from behind a rock and blindsided Ludwig, knocking him to the ground. He scrambled to his feet but was knocked down again by the lunging attacker, who wrapped his arms around Ludwig's legs. With Ludwig lying prone on the cave floor, the pirate slashed Ludwig before prying the seal from his hand.

"That's the second time I've taken this from you," the

man said as he looked up at Wilhelm. "I suggest you leave unless you want to end up like your friend here."

"Perhaps we can make another arrangement," Reinhard said as he stepped out of the shadows of the corridor. He nudged Captain Yang forward with a gun jammed into the side of her head.

"How about a trade," Reinhard said. "The seal for your captain's life?"

The man smiled and paced around. "You think you can come into our cave and threaten me, Captain Xi, into giving you this seal." Xi shook his head and chuckled. "Your arrogance is astounding, not to mention you think that I care about Captain Yang. She stole this gang from one of my best mates, and I swore to him that I'd get her back."

"You're lying," Wilhelm said.

"See if I care what you do to her," Xi said.

Wilhelm spun and threw his dagger at Captain Yang, hitting her in the chest. She gasped before falling forward and collapsing in a heap. He turned his attention to Xi, who didn't hesitate as he broke into a sprint. Reinhard fired once as Xi dove behind a pile of rocks.

The other pirates watching the scene unfold became enraged and stormed toward Reinhard and his unit. However, a hail of bullets met the attackers, sending them scurrying back to the outer edges of the cave.

Meanwhile, Wilhelm ran over to Yang and ripped out his dagger before taking off after Xi. The pirate appeared as if he would get away, scrambling up a craggy embankment only to slip. He slid down to the floor, where Wilhelm stood waiting.

"The terms of our deal have expired," Wilhelm said. "I'll be taking that seal now."

The pirate turned over and flung a mixture of dirt and

rocks into Wilhelm's face before attempting to escape again. However, Wilhelm dove after Xi and grabbed his feet, dragging him back down to the cave floor.

"The seal," Wilhelm said as he held out his hand.

Xi sighed and dug out the stone from his coat pocket. Wilhelm held it up and inspected it for a moment. As he did, Xi made an attempt to scramble up the hill again, but Wilhelm refused to allow it. He pounced on Xi and drove the dagger through his back, stabbing him three times before climbing off and standing up to address the rest of the onlookers.

"Go," Wilhelm said. "You owe your allegiance to no one now. And if you want to live, I suggest you not try to get in my way."

But not a single pirate moved.

"You have made a grave mistake," one of the pirates said from across the room. "And it will be your last."

CHAPTER 14

ONCE RICHARD AND HELEN REACHED SHALLOWER water, they jumped out and used the raft as cover from the pirates shooting at them. As they drew closer to the shore, Helen shot two of the pirates out of the trees, using only three shots to do it. Another pirate rushed onto the beach and signaled to the men. Richard counted four other men who scurried down to the ground and raced off into the forest.

After some eerie silence, Richard looked at Helen. "Is this some kind of trap?"

"Could be, but I don't see anyone else on the beach. Do you?"

Richard scanned the area but didn't see anyone. "Looks clear to me. What do you propose we do?"

"Let's go into the cave and see what the Reichswehr are up to."

The two agents hustled onto the shore, stopping only to get a few extra weapons from the men Helen had shot. Richard crouched low and stepped softly, straining to hear what was happening over the waves crashing just outside. A few seconds later, it was clear there was a gunfight in full swing.

Richard peered around a rock and saw half of Wilhelm's men hemmed in against a pile of rocks, dividing their attention between two groups of pirates in the expansive cavern. The groups exchanged sporadic gunfire.

"They must be getting low on ammunition," Richard said to Helen. "Wilhelm would have every single member of his unit firing if they weren't."

"Looks like we're a little late to the party," she said. "But that doesn't mean we can't still have some fun."

Helen pushed her way past Richard.

"What are you doing?" he asked. "We just can't go charging down there."

"Says who?"

Staying in the shadows, Richard followed after her around a corridor that appeared to circle the entire cave. However, she abruptly stopped.

"What is it?" Richard asked.

She nodded in the direction of a rock that jutted out from the wall where a young girl sat curled up in a fetal position crying softly.

"We need to talk to her," Richard said.

"You do it," Helen said. "I'm terrible with kids."

"You're just chicken," Richard said before he crept over to the girl, stopping a few feet away.

"Are you all right?" Richard asked.

The girl shook her head.

"What's your name?"

"Ti," she said and then sniffled.

"Well, Ti, can you tell me what's going on?"

"My uncle is dead," she said. "One of those men who attacked us in our cave killed him and took something from him. My mother told me it was going to make us all rich and we could move someplace normal. And maybe I could go to school."

Richard placed his hand gently on her shoulder. "Well,

Ti, I suggest you get out of here before anything else terrible happens. And my friend and I will do our best to punish those men for what they did to your uncle. How's that sound?"

She wiped away a few tears with the back of her hand and nodded.

"Do you know how to get out of here?" he asked.

She pointed behind her at a tunnel. "This is my secret way in and out."

"Well, get going," Richard said. "It's about to get real dangerous in here."

He stood up as she turned and darted out of sight.

"What did she say?" Helen asked.

"Wilhelm has the seal, but he's obviously hemmed in," Richard said. "And apparently he killed some guy."

Helen eyed the Reichswehr unit before turning to Richard. "I've got a plan. Come with me."

"You mind sharing that plan with me?"

"Just follow my lead."

Richard grabbed a fistful of her shirt as she tried to pull away. "I need to know what we're doing."

"Do you trust me?" Helen asked.

"Well, I—"

"Look, I don't have time to explain, but you'll figure everything out once we reach Wilhelm. Just stay behind me and go with me, okay?"

"Fine," Richard said. "But I want you to know I don't like being in the dark in situations like this."

"We're in a cave," she snapped. "Everyone's virtually in the dark."

Richard wasn't amused by Helen's reply, though in most normal circumstances he would've appreciated such wit.

They hustled along the corridor until they were directly

above the Reichswehr's position.

"Ready?" Helen asked.

"Not really since I don't know what—"

Helen tugged on his shirt, pulling him down the embankment with her.

The rocks trickling behind the Reichswehr position arrested Wilhelm's attention. He spun and turned to investigate. Once Richard made eye contact with the German, the look of curiosity on Wilhelm's face morphed into a sneer. He didn't put his hands in the air in a posture of surrender despite the fact that Helen had her gun trained on him.

"This isn't really a good time," Reinhard said. "Besides, if you're going to kill me, please go ahead. You'll both be marked by your government, forever, accused of restarting a war with Germany. Or you both might be gunned down before you get the chance."

Richard swallowed hard as the men who'd been firing at the pirates all turned their attention to him and Helen.

"Look," Helen began, "you've got something I want, and I've got something you want."

"And what's that?" Wilhelm asked.

"The seal of the realm in exchange for a way out of here."

Wilhelm grunted. "You don't think we can fight our way past these amateurs?"

Helen shrugged. "If you can, what are you still doing here?"

"I'm a wise tactician—it's the German way."

Her eyebrows shot upward. "How'd that work out for you in the Great War?"

Another bullet whistled in their direction. "I don't have time for this nonsense," Wilhelm said. "I suggest you make your way out before you end up dead yourself."

He turned his back on her and surveyed the pirates' two positions.

"I'm willing to give you something else," she said. "And it's far more valuable than a simple heirloom seal."

Wilhelm spun back around and wore a smirk on his face. "You have this object with you?"

She nodded. "I do."

"Then let's see it."

"You're looking at him," she said, gesturing toward Richard.

He scowled as he looked at his partner. "What are you doing?"

She ignored him and eyed Wilhelm. "Look, I have some harsh taskmasters as well. I understand the importance of bringing back what you were sent to get. However, if I ever had the opportunity to bring back something more valuable, something that would prove to be beneficial in the long term, I'd snatch up that offer as quickly as it was presented to me. Now, Richard is a valuable commodity in and of himself, something you know all too well. If it hadn't been for him, you'd already have two expensive artifacts to sell to beef up your poor military. But with him, perhaps you can do more. He knows where everything is hidden and has an uncanny ability to find things you'd never dreamed of finding. So, what do you say? A way out and Richard Halliburton for the seal?"

"Absolutely not," Wilhelm said as he turned back to face the pirates.

Richard watched Reinhard approach Wilhelm and have a brief but curt conversation. When they were finished, he turned around to address Helen.

"My commander here has persuaded me to take your offer provided that we can do with him whatever we like when we are finished with his services," Wilhelm said.

"Agreed," Helen said, shoving Richard over toward Wilhelm.

"If we don't make it out alive, our military will never receive the riches our country deserves," Wilhelm said as he took hold of Richard by his bicep.

"What are you doing?" Richard protested as he stared back at Helen. "No, I won't be a part of this, I—"

Wilhelm backhanded Richard, knocking him back a couple of steps and silencing him. "Rule number one in the Reichswehr: Never refuse to obey your commander."

Richard narrowed his eyes. "You're not my—"

Another slap across his face. "Don't make this difficult."

"The seal," Helen said, holding out her hand.

Wilhelm dug it out of his pocket. The artifact was wrapped up in a white rag. He opened it to show her the jade-colored stone. Richard gasped at the sight of the object.

Wilhelm turned to Richard. "Is there something you'd like to say about this stone?"

"It's just so—ordinary," Richard said. "I expected a seal that was believed to be a stamp of approval from the gods to look a little more—I don't know—royal."

"Are you suggesting that this is a fake?" Helen asked.

Richard shook his head. "I wouldn't begin to say such a thing. No one's seen it in nearly a thousand years. Who even knows what it really looks like?"

"We worked with a scientist who matched up the seal's marking with one known to be used by the emperors during the early eighth century," Wilhelm said. "We have already verified authenticity."

Richard scowled. "You're buying this, Helen?"

She kept her gun trained on Wilhelm as she glanced at

Richard. "He's fighting his way out of here with it. I doubt he'd be doing that if this wasn't the real thing."

"Where's this escape route?" Wilhelm asked.

She gave him directions to the tunnel she saw the little girl disappear into.

"If this is a trap, I'll hunt you down and kill you myself," Wilhelm said.

"If you don't trust me, you'll all be dead within the hour," she said. "I heard a couple of pirates talking outside that there are more reinforcements on the way."

Wilhelm gestured to his men. "Time to go."

Richard watched Helen pick her way up the slope. When she reached the top, she took cover behind a rock and looked at Richard.

"Trust me," she mouthed to him.

The only thing Richard felt was a tidal wave of betrayal. Helen had come up with a plan without consulting him and had given him over to the Reichswehr. No discussion. No request. No grand plan unveiled. A simple knife to the back.

"That's quite a partner you have," Wilhelm said after they hustled up the hill and took cover in the shadows of the corridor. The pirates continued to fire, bullets pinging all around the Germans.

A few minutes later, they reached the entrance to the tunnel.

"Is this it?" Wilhelm asked. "Because if it isn't, you're going to die with us."

Richard looked down and nodded. "This is the entrance. It'll dump us out a few feet above the water in the cove."

Wilhelm shoved Richard in the back. "Excellent. Now get moving."

CHAPTER 15

ELEN SECURED THE SEAL IN HER POCKET AND TOOK one last glance at Richard before climbing around a boulder and disappearing down the corridor. She felt a twinge of guilt for blindsiding him in such a manner, but it for his own good. While Richard possessed sufficient skills as an agent, she wasn't convinced he could act surprised enough if he was handed over to the Reichswehr on a whim. Springing such a move on him was cruel, but it was for the sake of his survival, she reasoned.

She wiped the sweat off her brow and continued to pick her way through the cave toward the exit. However, she didn't get far before she heard a roar from a large band of men.

Acting quickly, she found a nook to hide in as the men poured inside. The pirates had apparently been gathering reinforcements. She cringed as they raced back toward the center of the cave, knowing that Richard likely didn't stand a chance now. But any attempt to save him would be little more than a suicide mission. With the seal in her pocket, her own survival was contingent upon completing the mission.

She said a quick prayer for Richard under her breath and waited for the last of the pirates to pass by her position. Satisfied that they were all gone, she resumed her race toward the exit. However, when she reached daylight, she saw Ti sobbing on a rock.

Helen glanced into the cove and saw that the tide was coming in and that their boat appeared free from the sandbar. She eyed her raft, still tenuously beached about a hundred meters away. It was rocking as the ocean lapped farther and farther ashore.

"What's wrong, Ti?" Helen asked as she knelt next to the girl.

"It's my doll," she said. "It fell out of my hand when those men rushed by, and it's too far out in the water for me to get it."

"Where is it?" Helen asked, scanning for Ti's toy.

"There," Ti said, pointing near a clump of jagged rocks about thirty meters offshore.

"I'll get it for you," Helen said.

She couldn't bear the thought of the little girl not having her one comfort item to sleep with after the Reichswehr killed her uncle. Rushing into the water, Helen dove headlong into a wave and swam in the direction of the doll. Once she snagged it, she rushed back to Ti, reuniting her with the toy.

"Thank you," Ti said.

"You're welcome," Helen said. "Be safe."

She turned and sprinted toward her raft. However, just as she arrived at it, three pirates cut her off and seized the boat, shoving her back.

"Hey," Helen said. "That's my raft."

"Not anymore," one of the men said as he flashed a toothy grin.

"How am I supposed to get back to my boat?"

"You should've never come here in the first place," he said.

She took a few steps toward them and stopped as she stared at the trio.

Another one of the men brandished his gun. "That's far enough if you know what's good for you."

Helen stopped and sighed as she watched the men commandeer her best way to get back to the boat. She looked out at the Yen's boat. Lei and Shing were on the bow, waving for her to return. The five hundred-meter swim would be brutal, but she had no other alternative. After checking to make sure the seal was still secure, she ran into the ocean and started swimming.

As she fought her way through the choppy waters, she thought about Richard and hoped he was going to be okay. It was her way of assuaging a guilty conscience. She knew he'd be lucky to survive, though that was highly unlikely. If they somehow managed to escape, Wilhelm sounded as if he intended to kill Richard once the Reichswehr was finished with him.

At least it gives him a fighting chance.

She didn't want to think about it, knowing that she would hate anyone who put her in such a predicament. Perhaps he was still too green to know.

The mission is always the most important. We all know what we sign up for.

It was the thought she used to soothe her guilt. But it wasn't working. She'd figure out a way to get him back—if he somehow survived that onslaught.

Eventually, she reached the ship. Lei tossed down a rope ladder to help her climb aboard.

When she reached the deck, she wiped the water away from her face and looked around. Lei and Shing were the only people she could see.

"Where's your uncle?" she asked.

Lei chuckled. "He's down below taking care of some business."

"Did you get what you came for?" Shing asked.

She nodded. "In my pocket, safe and sound."

"Can we see it?" Lei asked.

She winced. "I don't know. This is the reason why I'm here. The reason why you're here is that boat right over there. Why haven't you retaken it yet?"

"We were hoping maybe you and your colleague would navigate it back to the harbor as you promised," Lei said.

"I thought you wanted to exact revenge on the Germans," she said.

"We also wanted our boat back," Shing said.

Helen sighed. "Well, can you at least get me a little closer? I'm worn out from that swim."

Lei glanced at Shing before directing his full attention back toward Helen. "Sure, but we really want to see the seal of the realm first."

She shook her head.

"Come on," Lei said. "We need to see it for ourselves. It'd be a great story to tell our friends."

"And trust me when I say this, but none of them would believe you," she said.

Shing eyed her closely. "I don't believe you have it."

"Yeah," Lei added. "And where's your colleague anyway? What happened to him?"

"He got hung up," she said. "I'll just wait for him on the other ship."

Lei shook his head. "My uncle won't like that too much. He's not going to trust you to just take the ship back to the harbor by yourself."

"You think I'm going to try and sail the seven seas in that fishing vessel?" she asked, pointing at the other boat. "I'll be lucky to make it back to the dock in once piece in that thing."

"Enough," Shing said as he brandished a gun. "Give me the seal now."

Helen raised her hands in a gesture of surrender. "What's going on here? Where's Yen?"

"Nobody has to get hurt," Shing said. "Just give me the seal, and I'll let you go."

Helen narrowed her eyes, glaring at the boy. He acted tough behind that gun, but if she saw him in a dark alley, he'd rue the day he crossed paths with her.

With a resigned sigh, she dug into her pocket and pulled out the seal. It was still covered up when she did.

"Unwrap it," Shing said, his weapon still trained on her.

Helen followed his orders, revealing the seal in all its glory.

"I guess you weren't lying," Shing said. "And for that, I'll spare your life."

He snatched the seal out of her hand.

"What now?" she said.

"You swim back to that other ship over there and return it to the harbor, or else we'll hunt you down," Lei said from behind Shing.

Deliberate footsteps fell with heavy thuds. Convinced that the two boys weren't capable of pulling off such a heist, Helen craned her neck to see who was behind the thieving. A man who wore similar clothing to the pirates she'd just encountered sauntered up next to the boys and put his arms around them both.

"Excellent work, gentlemen," he said. "You'll both make great pirates soon enough."

They smiled, soaking in the adulation from the apparent veteran. The man's graying hair was tied up in a ponytail, his right hand clutching a sheathed dagger.

"It's time for you to leave," the man said to Helen.

As she turned around, the man shoved her from behind with his foot.

Helen plunged into the water. She gasped for air as she resurfaced, shivering as she started to swim for the other vessel.

I don't remember the water being this cold a few minutes ago.

It was a thought she tried to ignore as she fell into rhythmic strokes through the ocean. Her sacrifice for Richard had been for nothing—and she wasn't sure she could ever forgive herself.

CHAPTER 16

RICHARD PUT ASIDE HELEN'S BETRAYAL AND FOCUSED on the task at hand. Scores of pirates wielding pistols and swords were pouring into the caves. While the first wave of combatants was still more than a minute away from reaching the Reichswehr unit, Richard realized there was no time to waste. However, Wilhelm held fast as he surveyed the landscape.

"What are you doing?" Richard said. "We need to leave now."

Wilhelm glared at his new prisoner. "The sooner your learn your place around here, the better for you."

Reinhard leaned close to Richard and spoke in a hushed tone. "He wants to draw them into the tunnels so we can kill them more easily. Our troops are rather skilled in navigating fights in these environments."

Richard wasn't inclined to let his survival be determined by the whims of an arrogant German general, one who had already proven his tactical skills were far from flawless. With the other soldiers preoccupied with the onslaught of approaching attackers, Richard considered making a dash down the corridor. He glanced to his right and was prepared to run before he saw about twenty pirates racing toward them.

"We need to go now," Richard said, tugging on Wilhelm's sleeve.

Wilhelm drew his hand back to smack Richard but stopped short when he noticed the ambush. "We must go now," Wilhelm shouted.

The Reichswehr unit fell in line behind Wilhelm and scurried toward the corridor Helen had told them about. Richard stayed near the front with Wilhelm and was guarded by Reinhard, who had been instructed to keep their captive alive at all cost.

Less than a minute later, the first band of pirates reached the Germans. The fight was a short one as the Reichswehr troops were as good as advertised by Reinhard. They made quick work of the ragtag group of men who'd failed to catch their invaders by surprise.

However, the brief battle still took time, a commodity Wilhelm and his men were in short supply of if they intended to escape.

Wilhelm wanted to take his customary inventory, assessing if they had any losses or injuries. But Reinhard urged Wilhelm forward.

"They're going to be on us any second now," Reinhard said. "And we're not carrying enough supplies to endure a long attack. We need to head to the water right now."

Wilhelm nodded and ordered the men to follow him. He broke into a sprint, navigating the dim tunnel with precision and speed. Meanwhile, his troops fell in line and mimicked his skill and urgency in moving through the corridor.

Despite their proven competency, Richard could hear the pirates gaining on them. And with no way of knowing how much farther they needed to travel to reach the cove, he decided to speak up again.

"Sir," Richard said to Wilhelm as they ran, "we're going to be overwhelmed."

"I'm not sure you're going to be all that useful with your keen observations," Wilhelm snapped. "Not another word."

"I know how we can stop them," Richard said. "It'll give you enough time to make your escape."

"And how do you intend to do that?"

"Block the path behind us," Richard suggested.

Wilhelm shook his head. "With what? Bodies?"

Richard nodded.

"No, it's too risky," Wilhelm said.

"Not if you know what you're doing."

"And you do?"

Richard chuckled. "I think you're well aware of what I'm capable of. I've got quite an arm."

"Even the best arm might still suffer quite a bit of residual from the bomb," Wilhelm said. "And who's to say you won't run off with the pirates? I already traded everything for you. I'm not about to let you out of my sight."

Reinhard interrupted. "I'll stay with him, sir."

"Are you sure?" Wilhelm asked.

"As sure as I can be in a situation like this."

"Very well then," Wilhelm said. "Work fast."

"I just need one of your Mills bombs," Richard said.

"Not on your life," Wilhelm said.

"We'll all be dead if you don't," Richard said. "You just have to trust me. Apparently, your second in command already does."

"Fine," Wilhelm said. "Someone give Mr. Halliburton a Mills bomb."

"Actually, I'd like two, just in case something goes wrong with the first one," Richard said.

Wilhelm sighed. "Reinhard if he tries anything suspicious, shoot him."

Reinhard nodded before he and Richard fell to the back

of the line. Richard explained that he needed to wait until they reached the right spot to ambush the pirates with the bombs. Once Richard identified an ideal location—one around a corner after a long straight stretch—he prepared to throw the grenade.

"Are you sure this is going to work?" Reinhard asked.

"There's only one way to find out," Richard said, crouching low behind a small boulder.

At that moment, he sprang from his spot and hurled a grenade into a pack of men before diving back behind the shielding rock. When Richard stepped back into the open again, he saw bodies littered all over the cave floor—but more pirates were stepping over them.

Richard cocked his arm and flung his other grenade at the other men, who collapsed to the ground with the explosion.

Several men fought their way through. Without another grenade to toss, Richard picked up a nearby rock and launched it toward the men. This time, they dove to the ground.

"Let's go," Richard said as he spun on his heel and raced after the rest of the Reichswehr soldiers. Reinhard remained right behind his hostage, reminding him of what might happen if he attempted to escape.

They worked their way back to the front with Wilhelm, reporting the success of their mission.

"I must admit I'm surprised to see you again," Wilhelm said. "I thought those savages would carve you up."

"My father used to always say, 'Never count out a Halliburton,'" Richard said. "And now you know why."

"We're not free yet," Wilhelm said, "though I believe the entrance is just ahead. That looks like daylight to me, does it not?"

Richard nodded. "Sure does."

As they neared the opening, Richard squinted as he tried to adjust to the sunrays beaming into the tunnel. He held his eyes up to shield the light when he noticed the silhouette of a man leaping out from behind a boulder.

"Look out!" he shouted.

An alert Wilhelm was able to turn in time to stop the attacker. However, there was another one lurking behind the same rock. He jumped out and stormed toward Reinhard with a knife. Richard lowered his shoulder and knocked the man into the side of the craggy wall. He stumbled for a moment allowing Richard time to kick the man in the face, knocking him out.

Reinhard looked at Richard and then glanced down at the unconscious pirate. "He could've killed me."

"Well, don't start thinking we're best friends," Richard said. "My chance at survival depends upon yours."

Once the entire team reached the opening, they could see their situation. The raft they used to get ashore was gone, but the ship was still moored in the cove about fifty meters away. One of the soldiers left on board signaled for them to hurry.

One by one, the men leaped feet first into the water. Richard waited until everyone, but he and Reinhard remained.

"Your turn," Reinhard said.

Richard took a few steps back before racing to the edge and diving headlong into the water. His long strokes sliced through the water more rapidly than all the soldiers who'd gone before him. When he reached the ship, the lone German agent aboard dropped a rope ladder for Richard. He scampered up to the deck and waited as the troops filed up until Wilhelm brought up the rear.

Wilhelm glanced back at the water and saw pirates

streaming out of the cave, opening and jumping into the water then swimming toward the boat.

"We don't have much time, but I want to tell you something very important," he said.

Richard's lips curled at the edges, anticipating Wilhelm to thank his new prisoner for saving the troops. Richard placed his hands behind his back and tilted his head back, preparing to absorb the praise.

"Some of you may have questions about why I would make such a trade, exchanging the seal for this man, Mr. Richard Halliburton," Wilhelm said as he strode around the deck. "But I think we now all know why that deal was struck."

Richard's grin spread as Wilhelm continued.

"However, there's something I want you to understand very clearly."

Before another word was uttered, Richard felt a fist furiously collide with his face. He tottered for a moment before crashing to the deck, knocked out cold.

CHAPTER 17

HELEN LOOKED ACROSS THE COVER TO SEE THE Germans spilling into the bay. She watched one of the final men dive headfirst into the water, resulting in a brief chuckle. The scene momentarily assuaged her conscience.

At least he's still alive.

And as much as she wanted to signal to him, she refrained. Without any way to fight back, the Germans could descend upon her and do whatever they wished to her, an unpleasant thought she quickly dismissed.

Helen's head bobbed just above the surface while she was treading water and searching for alternate transportation. Near the entrance to the cove, she noticed a sailboat moored twenty meters offshore. With no one apparently watching it or preparing to use it, she swam in the vessel's direction. By the time she reached it, the Germans were heading back in the direction of Hong Kong.

She took a few seconds to rest her arms before pulling herself up on the side of the boat. However, when she did, she was surprised to see a pair of men sitting inside.

"Do you need help?" one of the men asked.

Helen froze, unsure if she wanted to finish climbing in. "Yes, I do. Those men over there stole our ship and flung me out into the water. I need to get back to that ship."

One of the men cocked his head to one side and eyed her carefully. "So you swam to our ship?"

"Do you see any other boats that could keep pace with that fishing trawler over there?" she asked, pointing toward the Reichswehr's stolen ship while she remained bobbing in the ocean.

The two men looked at each other flashing a quick knowing glance before nodding in unison and agreeing to assist her in her pursuit of the other vessel. They each grabbed one of Helen's arms and yanked her aboard.

"What were you doing in this area?" the other man asked. "This is a dangerous place for a woman."

"It's not something I really want to talk about right now," she said, proceeding cautiously with the two strangers. "But let's just say if I knew then what I know now, I never would've ventured to this cove."

"The only reason we visit this place is because of the fishing," the other man said. "It's a good place to get everything you have stolen if the pirates decide they want to plunder your boat."

"There must be great fishing here then," she said, forcing a smile.

"The best," the man said as he gestured to a pile of fish.

Helen nodded as she glanced at the haul spilling across the deck. However, she stopped quickly when she noticed that there was something stuffed into the mouth of each fish.

A few minutes later, they were pulling up the anchor and hoisting the sails. They skimmed across the water in the same general direction as the Reichswehr vessel.

"Where are you headed now?" Helen asked.

"The same place as that trawler—the Hong Kong harbor," said the man, who was captaining the boat.

After a half-hour, their pace slowed as they took a route

that seemed equidistant from both the island's shoreline and the rest of China. Helen tried not to act frustrated at the diminishing speed, but she realized that the men might not have as much urgency if she didn't say something.

"Is there any way we can make this ship go faster?" she asked. "I really need to be close to the harbor when that boat docks so I'll have a fighting chance of catching up with them."

"Unfortunately, that's not how it works on this type of boat, lady," the captain said. "We're all at the mercy of the wind."

She glowered at him. "What do you take me for? A complete and utter fool? I've probably sailed more hours already in my life than you'll ever do, so quit pretending like I'm some helpless woman and don't try to placate me."

The other man sauntered over to her and sat down right next to her. She scooted away but couldn't get far after he placed his hand on her leg and clamped down on it. With a strong tug, he yanked her back next to him.

"Where are you going?" he said. "We're not going anywhere, but I've got a few ideas about how we can pass the time."

Helen looked over her shoulder at the other man, who was lumbering toward them with a mischievous grin on his face. Immediately, she recognized that her odds would be better in a one-on-one situation with each man instead of getting double-teamed. She pulled up her pants leg and reached for the ankle holster that housed her knife. Ripping it loose, she slashed the throat of the man next to her. She pushed him to the deck as he struggled to stop the bleeding.

The other man who'd been walking toward her stopped about ten feet away. He looked down and grabbed a rope that had a grappling hook attached to it. Whipping it around a

136 | GARRETT DRAKE

few times, he unleashed it in Helen's direction. She slid aside, avoiding the claw. Then she snatched it off the ground and slung it around the boat's mast. The hook swung around several times before it dug into the wood and remained stuck there.

Helen rushed toward the man, who readied himself with his feet shoulder-width apart and his arms open to grab her. But instead of running straight into him as he had anticipated, she slid headfirst along the deck and stabbed him in the leg as she passed by. Crippled by the cut, the man's knees buckled as he fell down. Unwilling to let the fight drag out any longer than necessary, Helen grabbed the rope and swung around the mast before delivering a driving kick to the man's face and knocking him out.

Once she settled back onto the deck, she looked over at the one man who had obviously bled out. Hurrying to secure them both, she threw the dead man on top of the unconscious one and tied them together with some rope and affixed the anchor to them. Then she leveraged their bodies upright and tipped them over the edge, sending them splashing into the ocean. They floated for a moment until the anchor pulled taut and dragged them well beneath the surface.

Helen collapsed on the deck, exhausted from the fight. She'd been so focused on her own survival that she didn't see another trawler approaching her until it had drawn alongside her boat. She dipped a bucket into the water and splashed the deck in an attempt to wash off the blood that had pooled nearby.

"Ma'am," asked a man who was wearing a monocle and leaning on the railing of his ship, "are you all right?"

"I'm fine," she said, forcing a smile.

"Well, it's just that we don't see many women out here

alone sailing a boat. Did something happen?"

Helen glanced at her feet and moved them to hide most of the remaining stain. "Nope," she said as she shook her head, "it's just your regular day at sea. Lots of wind and sun, but not necessarily when and how you want it."

The man was draped in a trench coat and stroked his chin as he studied Helen's boat. "Is this your ship?"

"For now, it is," she said. "I borrowed it from someone earlier today. I'm on my way back to the harbor to return it."

"I see," the man said. He shot a look at one of the men nearby who nodded subtly.

"Is there anything else I can help you with?" Helen asked.

The bespectacled man nodded and pulled his coat back, revealing a gun. "As a matter of fact, there is, Agent Williams."

CHAPTER 18

RICHARD AWOKE WITH A POUNDING HEADACHE AND bound to a chair with ropes. He slowly scanned the room to get his bearings. Based on the droning hum from just outside the door and the slight tossing motion, he deduced that he was still on the Reichswehr's stolen fishing trawler. But where exactly was a question he couldn't answer. For all he knew, he could be on his way to Singapore or Sydney.

A half-hour later, a pair of soldiers delivered a plate of food to him consisting of a couple of pieces of bread and an apple along with a glass of water. One of the men removed the bindings and collected them, while the other slid the tray onto a nearby table.

"Can either of you tell me what's happening?" Richard asked. "Where am I? Where's Wilhelm?"

They both ignored him and promptly exited, locking the door behind them.

Richard devoured the food and wondered how long he'd been out. He hadn't realized how hungry he was until he finished eating. Searching around the room, he found little more than some first aid supplies and a mop.

He paced around for a few minutes, contemplating how he might escape given the opportunity. However, a firm knock on the door interrupted his internal deliberations.

Without waiting for Richard's reply, two armed Reichswehr agents entered the room along with Wilhelm.

"You have a funny way of repaying a guy for saving the life of one of your troops," Richard said.

Wilhelm grunted. "If we're keeping a ledger, you remain in quite a bit of debt to me, so please dispense with the notion that I owe you any favors. Besides, the biggest favor I'm doing for you right now is keeping you alive."

"You can always cut me loose and see how I'll do on my own."

Wilhelm huffed a soft laugh through his nose. "I doubt you'd want me to toss you overboard right now into the South China Sea. You'd be dead in a few hours unless you possess some superhuman ability to swim miles and miles in the ocean without drowning."

"How many miles are we talking about?"

Wilhelm waved dismissively at him. "I didn't come down here to humor you. In fact, I have a very serious question for you."

"Ask away. I've obviously got nothing but lots of free time on my hands since you've locked me away here on your ship."

Wilhelm crossed his arms and leaned against the wall. "How much is the seal of the realm worth?"

"Depends on who you ask."

"I'm asking you," Wilhelm said as he glared at Richard.

"I've heard anywhere from half a million pounds to five million. I guess at the end of the day, it's like everything else. It's worth whatever someone is willing to pay for it."

"And what would you pay for it?"

Richard chuckled. "Well, if I had that type of money as a private collector, I might pay around two to three million for it. But that's pure speculation."

Wilhelm clapped his hands and rubbed them together. "Excellent. That's what I wanted to hear to affirm my decision."

"Interesting. I had no idea I had so much influence on you. Could I perhaps persuade you to tell me what I'm doing here and where we're going?"

Wilhelm shook his head. "You don't need to know everything, just what I tell you."

Richard was quiet for a moment before breaking the silence. "If you have big plans for me, you might want to bring me on now in the formulation stage so we're not surprised by something you didn't think of."

"My men are the best soldiers in the world and leave no stone unturned as they get ready for a mission," Wilhelm said.

"With all due respect, it's my life on the line, not yours, if you plan to do something with me."

"That's the price you pay for trying to stop me. And if you cross me again, I can assure you that the situation you're about to walk into will carry far graver consequences than being my lackey for a few missions."

Richard sighed. "So what do you want me to do?"

"I want you to retrieve the seal for me."

"You're just going to send me out to my old partner—"

"The one who double-crossed you," Wilhelm interjected.

"Yes, the one who double-crossed me, and I'm just going to saunter up to her and ask her for the seal?"

"Of course not," Wilhelm said. "She doesn't even have it anymore."

"And you know this how?"

Wilhelm smiled wryly. "Mr. Halliburton, you were given one of our special Reichswehr sedatives after you were rendered unconscious. An entire day has gone by, and during that time, we learned that the pirates have recaptured the seal. We happened upon a pirate who'd been cast away. We gave him some earnest money and promised him ten times that amount if he could report back to us any information that would lead to the whereabouts of the seal. We dropped him into a life raft, and he was picked up by several fellow pirates who told him that they had captured the seal back from an American woman. This morning, he reported the news to us. His dead body is in the room next door."

Richard winced. "So you want to storm the cave again and retake the seal from the pirates?"

"Of course not," Wilhelm said. "That's a messy proposition. I have a far neater plan, but it requires your services since apparently everyone is on the lookout for a group of German soldiers."

"You're going to send me back in there alone?"

"Wrong again, Mr. Halliburton. You see, I learned a long time ago that sometimes it's easier to let someone else do all the work for you and then swoop in at the last moment to take it all for yourself."

Richard furrowed his brow. "So what exactly is the mission?"

"We know who the pirates are going to use for fencing the artifact," Wilhelm said. "And you're going to pose as a potential buyer. We'll handle the rest of the details from there. Think you can handle such a menial task?"

"Sounds like a very important one, one that requires my help to be successful."

"If you want to live, I urge you to take this assignment very seriously and resist the notion that you can be the hero. My suggestion is that you resign yourself to failing your superior's assignment. If you fail, the consequences will be dire."

Richard took a deep breath before exhaling slowly. "Whatever you need me to do, I'll do it."

"That's more like it," Wilhelm said. "If you maintain this attitude, we'll make great partners."

Wilhelm nodded knowingly at his two guards, who retied Richard to the chair. Then the Germans all exited the room, leaving Richard alone with his thoughts.

"Resign myself to failure?" Richard said beneath his breath. "Not a chance."

CHAPTER 19

ELEN TOOK A STEP BACK FROM THE MAN AS HE
boarded her sailboat. She wondered if she needed
to whip out her knife and deal with him in the same
manner as the previous owners of the boat. But she decided
to wait and see what he wanted to discuss. With both of his
hands jammed into his pockets, he paced back and forth for
a moment before speaking again.

"You missed a spot," the man said, glancing down at
Helen's feet.

She looked down. "What are you talking about?"

"Let me cut to the chase, Ms. Williams, and spare you
your dignity," he said. "My name is Shawn Lee, and I work
for the Ministry of the Interior. I recently had a conversation
with someone I think you know, a Mr. Hank Foster. You do
know him, don't you?"

If Mr. Lee knew this much about her and her boss, the
question had to be a rhetorical one. But she managed a feeble
nod nonetheless.

"He warned me that someone was making an attempt
to steal the heirloom seal of the realm, which has been lost
for nearly a thousand years and has become more or less a
myth in our nation. Have you seen this seal before?"

She nodded. "Of course, I have. But you probably
already knew that. In fact, I had it in my possession a few

hours ago until I was ambushed at gunpoint and forced to hand it back to a pirate commanding a ship I was supposed to be navigating back to the Hong Kong harbor."

"I see," Lee said. "Well, I must say that the thought of anyone profiting off an artifact that once belonged to the great dynasties of this country makes my blood boil. But I get even more upset when I consider the fact that it might be a group of foreigners who take something so important in China's history and use it for their own gain. It's disgusting. Don't you agree?"

"That's why I'm here. Otherwise, I would be in some other part of the world trying to stop someone else from doing some dastardly deed."

Lee smiled. "Then we share a common goal."

"Unfortunately, I'm not sure there's anything I can do to help you," she said. "I'm only one person, incapable of fighting those men on my own. And at the moment, I'm down a partner."

"So I see," he said. "What happened?"

Helen sighed. "I don't really want to talk about it right now."

"Is he dead?"

"That's not something I can answer with any degree of certainty right now. I just now that when I left him, he was alive yet in the hands of those ruthless Germans."

"Where do you think the seal is now?"

She shrugged. "Your guess is as good as mine, though I must admit that it's not my first concern at the moment. I'm more worried about my partner and his whereabouts."

"What if I told you that you could save both him and help me? Would you be interested?"

Helen's eyebrows shot upward as she cocked her head to one side. "What exactly do you know?"

"I know where he is and how you can get him back."

"But there's a catch, isn't there?"

"The only catch is that you have to retake the seal and deliver it to me so I can keep it safe from those dastardly European marauders," he said. "And in the process, you'll be able to help your partner escape the clutches of the Reichswehr. What do you say?"

"If you're seeking my help, I assume this assignment will be fraught with danger?"

"Depends on how you define danger."

"I suppose what I'm really asking is what kind of support will I have?"

"None," he said. "Other than setting up the meeting with the man who'll be in possession of the seal in a matter of days, you'll be on your own. Up for the challenge?"

She nodded. "I'm all for anything that will help me keep that artifact out of the hands of the Germans. Saving my partner isn't a bad result either."

"I thought you might say that."

Helen eyed him closely as he adjusted his monocle. "I do have a question for you."

"Ask away."

"Why wouldn't you use legal methods to seize the seal?"

Lee nodded. "That is a good question. Mr. Shufu has been instrumental in bringing many new teams here to search for ancient artifacts. And it's become a lucrative business for the government. Prosecuting him would damage his reputation and potentially disrupt the steady stream of organizations coming here to dig."

"So if I agree to work with you, what is the next step?"

Lee strode over toward the port side where his boat was now tethered to hers with a small ramp. He offered his right hand, gesturing with his left for her to come near to him.

"We have far nicer accommodations aboard our vessel," he said. "Let's get you all cleaned up along with a good night's sleep, and then we'll discuss all the details in the morning. How does that sound?"

"Well—" she said before pausing.

"Did I mention that my ship has an onboard chef? You look like you could use a good meal."

Helen took his hand and stepped up onto the plank thrown across the two ships. "You've done your research."

Lee grinned. "Of course. I know how fond you are of fine food. We even have a nice selection of wine, impressive, even considering the circumstances."

Helen left behind the sailboat and stared out across the horizon. She was hopeful again, confident that she just might be able to correct her biggest mistake and retrieve the seal—all in one fell swoop.

CHAPTER 20

RICHARD CLOSED HIS EYES AND TRIED TO IGNORE THE constant thrumming of the engine from the trawler chugging through the choppy waters. Confined to such a small space, there wasn't much for him to do other than sit and think. And that activity had become a dangerous one for him. He needed to get out for more than his permitted three breaks to use the toilet at the end of the hall. Richard needed sunshine.

After he devoured the breakfast delivered to his makeshift prison cell, he was about to knock to get the guard's attention and hand over a tray with the empty dishes when the door swung open. Reinhard strode in and held a couple of teacups, the steam drifting lazily upwards from them.

"Do you take cream in your tea?" Reinhard asked.

With mouth agape, Richard stared at the German. "Are you offering me some?"

"There isn't anyone else crammed into this room, is there?"

"I—I don't really like tea," Richard admitted.

"Nonsense," Reinhard said. "There are only two kinds of people in this world as it relates to tea. Those who love tea and those who will fall in love with it."

"I'm American, not English, remember?"

"How could I forget? Perhaps you'd like some of that disgusting juice squeezed from coffee beans instead."

"That's not how it—oh, never mind."

"Here," Reinhard said, offering the cup to Richard, "you must try this. It's absolutely divine."

Richard wrapped both hands around the warm mug and brought it closer to his lips. The spices emanating from the drink tickled his nose.

"Is this cinnamon?" Richard asked.

"Yes," Reinhard said, "straight from Saigon. The absolute best cinnamon in the world."

Richard took a sip and was delighted by the flavor. "My, this is quite different."

"Good, isn't it?" Reinhard asked.

Richard nodded. "So, why are you giving this to me?"

"Let's take a walk up on the deck," Reinhard said.

Richard didn't need to hear the suggestion again. As he emerged into the sunlight, he stopped and closed his eyes, letting the rays dance upon his face for a moment before continuing after Reinhard. He led them to the ship's bow and leaned forward on the railing. The casual way Reinhard handled the encounter made Richard feel as though they were friends—almost. Behind them, two armed Reichswehr soldiers stood, keeping a keen eye on the conversation.

Richard returned his attention to Reinhard and studied him for a moment before speaking. "What's this really all about?"

"I figured a man like you wouldn't enjoy being caged up in the darkness for that long," Reinhard said. "We all need to see the sun every once in a while."

"That's all?"

"And I wanted to thank you for saving my life. Wilhelm isn't very forgiving and can be a difficult man to get along with, even when you're on his side. But when you're not, you will find yourself wishing you were never born."

"I guess I'm somewhere in the middle then," Richard said.

Reinhard chuckled. "Wilhelm hates you, but he also recognizes that you could become a valuable asset for the Reichswehr."

"As much as I find these ventures exhilarating, I'm not interested in aligning with the German military."

Reinhard took a deep breath and exhaled slowly. He drained the rest of his tea and then pointed out at the surrounding environment in a sweeping gesture with his hand.

"Look at all this," Reinhard said. "You're now in Hangchow, one of the most beautiful places in all of China. And it's a peaceful trip, one where you don't have to worry about looking over your shoulder at someone chasing you."

"The only reason that isn't the case is because you've captured me. If I'm not pursuing you, rest assured the allies will find someone else who will."

"And we'll handle them just like we've handled you. You're alive—for now. And there's still time for you to join forces with the Reichswehr. We'd make a great team."

"While this all sounds terribly inviting, I'm afraid that's I'm not willing to betray my country like that."

"Who said anything about betrayal?" Reinhard asked. "All we want you to do is help us get our hands on these precious artifacts. And did I mention what we'd be willing to pay you?"

Richard shook his head. "You've kept that part a secret so far."

"We'd offer you double whatever the American government is paying you."

"That's rather generous, but that's not what I want to do with my life."

Reinhard laughed. "And from what I know about you,

you didn't want to be a spy your whole life either. From the report I've read about you, your lifelong dream is to be a travel writer, experiencing adventure and then writing about it."

"That's actually accurate."

"But you're not doing that."

"Maybe my dream isn't so cut and dry at the moment. There are other things I enjoy doing, things I need to be doing, things I feel compelled to do."

"Like risk your life so some bureaucrat can get elected?"

Richard drew back and gawked at Reinhard's response. "You almost sound like an American with that comment. Are you sure you haven't spent any time in the United States?"

Reinhard shook his head and grinned. "Political corruption isn't something you Americans have cornered. We've got plenty of centuries' worth of experience more than you. You might have a different constitution, but greed and the thirst for power are common vices. Quite frankly, it's why we're both out here."

"That's not exactly how I see things," Richard said. "I think that—"

"I didn't invite you up here to debate about our countries' political dispositions. To be honest, I mostly wanted to tell you thank you for saving my life back in that cave."

Richard shrugged. "We all might have common vices, but common decency is a thing too. You've been kind to me, and for that I'm grateful."

Reinhard nodded knowingly. "There's also a third reason I wanted to speak with you."

"A third reason?"

"Yes, I wanted to test your knowledge of tea."

"I suppose I failed miserably then," Richard said. "Does this relate to my upcoming assignment?"

"You're going to meet with Lu Shufu tomorrow morning posing as Gerard Williams, an American broker working for an antiquities dealer from Germany, and you need to be able to entice him to sell you the seal."

"How am I supposed to do that?"

"Just pique his interest about meeting with a prospective buyer and give him our offer. If that doesn't intrigue him, we have other means to capture the seal. I'll give you all the details later. But just remember, Shufu is a tea connoisseur. He's a cold man, so if you have a difficult time relating to him, tea is your way in."

"But I don't know anything about tea in China other than the fact that they make lots of it."

"Tell him about American tea."

"But I don't know anything about that either," Richard said.

"Then make it up. I just really need you to succeed."

"Why is this assignment so important to you? The way you said that, it almost sounds like this is personal."

"It is," Reinhard said. "My wife died during this mission, and I haven't been home yet. And Wilhelm refuses to go back until he has something in hand to give General Seeckt, who's very unforgiving. So, yes, it's incredibly personal. Just get Shufu to sell it, will you?"

"I'll do my best."

* * *

THE NEXT MORNING, Richard adjusted his tie as he hustled along the sidewalk toward the meeting place with the artifacts dealer Lu Shufu. The restaurant selected for the encounter was situated along the fertile banks of the Qiantang River. So captivated was Richard by the setting that he wished he could continue strolling along for hours. However, the two armed Reichswehr soldiers following him assured that he wouldn't miss his appointment.

Shufu was the only patron in the restaurant, seated at a table on the patio overlooking the water. He was pouring steaming hot water into a cup when Richard approached.

"Mr. Shufu," Richard said. "I'm—"

"I know who you are, Mr. Williams," Shufu said, gesturing toward the seat across from him. "Let's keep this brief. I have a busy day today."

Shufu didn't look up at Richard while slicing through a piece of bread and slathering it with butter. The wire-rimmed glasses hung just off the end of his nose, while a bowler hat covered all but a few streaks of graying hair that poked from beneath the rim. Before taking a bite of his breakfast, Shufu checked his watch and then looked up and locked eyes with Richard.

"Well, come on, lad," Shufu said in his British accent. "I don't have all day."

Richard nodded. "Oh, yes, right. Well, I don't like to do any business until I've had a cup of tea in the morning. And this morning, I've been unable to accomplish that."

"That is a problem we must remedy immediately," Shufu said. He snatched the mug sitting in front of Richard and quickly prepared some tea.

"Thank you," Richard said as he collected the mug and took a sip. "My, this is far better than what we have back home."

"Welcome to China, Mr. Williams. If I'd had any sense, I would've become a tea exporter instead of dealing in ancient artifacts."

"They both require refined taste, don't they?" Richard said.

"Something that's lacking in the new world from what I hear."

Richard shrugged. "Well, there's certainly no one who's

figured out how to make great tea yet. But I happen to know some people who have expensive taste in antiquities. And one particular client of mine from Europe is interested in an item you recently acquired."

Shufu stroked his chin and looked Richard up and down. "I don't have anything new in my inventory, but suppose I did. How did you learn about this and get here so quickly?"

"I was already here on other business when I was messaged by my client. So, I decided to maximize my time. Being wise has taken me far in this world."

"Well, I'm sorry to disappoint you, but I truly don't have anything new to sell you."

"The buyer I represent is convinced you do."

"Then your buyer would be wrong."

Richard eyed him cautiously. "Are you sure you didn't get the seal of the realm in a recent transaction? My buyer is offered to pay you one lump sum of eight million pounds."

Shufu sat upright and shifted in his seat. "Did you say the seal of the realm?"

"You heard correct."

"And did you say eight million pounds?"

"Eight million pounds," Richard repeated.

"In that case, I might know where to find such a rare and sought-after object."

"Good," Richard said. "My buyer's offer will expire at midnight." He slid a piece of paper across the table to the dealer. "That's the address where you can meet me to make the exchange. The offer will expire at midnight—and good luck getting anyone else to pay that exorbitant of a price for the seal."

"If I can get my hands on it, I'll be there," Shufu said. "But it won't be easy, so—how do you Americans say it— don't hold your breath?"

Richard smiled and winked. "I have full confidence in your skills. I'll see you at that address later today."

He stood and exited the restaurant. After walking a few blocks, he turned around to look for the Reichswehr guards, who were still behind him and keeping an eye on him from a distance. For a fleeting moment, Richard considered running. He figured he could elude them. But before he could make a move, he felt a hand clamp down on his wrist. He shot a glance to his right and saw Reinhard.

"How'd it go?" he asked.

"It sounded promising, though he acted as if he didn't have the item," Richard said.

"Of course, he'd have to. Otherwise, if he tipped someone that he possessed the artifact, he'd have to be aware that thieves would swarm his office in search of the seal."

"I guess we'll find out before midnight."

* * *

RICHARD SAT ON the floor in his hotel room, reading a copy of Charles Dickens' A Tale of Two Cities in English, the only piece of literature he found that wasn't written in another language. He was sipping a cup of cinnamon tea, if only for appearances when Shufu finally arrived at his door.

Richard checked his watch. There were only ten minutes left until the deal supposedly expired.

He nearly jumped three feet off the floor when he heard a knock at his door.

CHAPTER 21

WILHELM PACED AROUND HIS HOTEL ROOM, blurting out his thoughts in short bursts to Reinhard, who was seated in a velvet armchair in the corner. While Wilhelm would've preferred his top officer to offer some feedback, he remained silent as Wilhelm opined about everything, sometimes ranting and other times raving about the motherland. Despite his plethora of sentiments, Wilhelm always came back to one central tenant: Germany could only succeed with military might. It was an ideal he shared with General Seeckt, which was the driving force for this mission.

Wilhelm peeked through the blinds onto the dark street below and then up at the hotel across the street. "Can't we just send a couple of men over to Shufu's house and steal the seal?"

"Just be patient, sir," Reinhard said. "That's still an option, but only if he doesn't show up tonight."

"And you're confident that he'll show?"

"Based on my conversation with Mr. Halliburton, I'll be surprised if he doesn't. I'm sure it's not every day that he stumbled upon an artifact that's worth eight million pounds."

Wilhelm stepped away from the window and resumed pacing around the room. "Of course, but the seal isn't worth that much either. What if that price makes him suspicious?"

"It might seem high enough to arouse some suspicion, but what is that you always tell me about greed and mankind?"

"Men are inherently greedy, especially businessmen. There's always enough, but they never believe it."

"What does that say about us then?" Reinhard asked.

"We're wise—because we know how to utilize greed for our purposes, which are ultimately for the greater good. Otherwise, the world will soon devolve into a society where the weak can rule the strong. Everyone has their place, and they must realize that."

"In other words, the end we seek justifies our means to get there."

Wilhelm snapped. "Precisely. Understanding greed is far better than simply wallowing in it. If we know how to leverage it for our purposes, all the better. The world will be better with a powerful nation that can help enforce the kind of ideals that make our society stronger."

Wilhelm had more to say, but his pontificating was interrupted when the door flew open and Erich Krause, one of the unit's intelligence specialists, raced inside.

"Pardon the intrusion, sir, but this just couldn't wait," Krause said.

"What on earth happened? Is it the seal?" Wilhelm asked.

"No, sir. That's the least of our worries at the moment. I'm afraid we're about to be under siege."

"Under siege? By who?"

"By our own," Krause said. "I was down at the docks checking on our ship and securing some more supplies for our journey home when I noticed a boat pull into the harbor that had German markings on it. I decided to see who else from the motherland might be in Hangchow at the same time as us and almost immediately, I recognized some of the men on board."

"It's General Seeckt, isn't it?"

Krause shook his head. "Not exactly, but they're from the Schwarz Reichswehr."

"So, Seeckt sent his special elite unit after us," Reinhard said. "I guess we should feel honored."

"You're not going to feel anything but pain when they come knocking," Wilhelm said. "They run around the world on assignment for his personal vendettas."

"Apparently, we're one of those now," Krause said. "I overheard one of the men say that Seeckt was upset he hadn't heard from us in so long, but it was too late now."

"It's a waste of time to give him a report that we're still out here doing our job without anything else of value to give him," Wilhelm said. "I told him the last time I spoke with him that I'd let him know when we had something to report."

"Maybe he's tired of funding our expeditions," Reinhard said. "He could always just call us home."

"That's not how Seeckt operates," Wilhelm said. "If you don't live up to his expectations, he expects you to be eliminated until he finds someone who can do what he wants, no matter how unrealistic that assignment is."

"How many are there?" Reinhard asked. "And do they know where we are?"

"I counted six men," Krause said. "But as far as our location goes, it's hard to tell, but we haven't exactly been invisible here. We are foreigners, after all, and anyone who's asked if they've seen a group of Germans will likely mention us. With a cursory investigation, they should be able to find us rather quickly."

"But tonight?" Wilhelm asked. "We have another operation we're in the middle of."

"I'd be ready for anything, sir," Krause said.

Wilhelm buried his face in his hands for a moment before continuing. "If they interfere with our mission to get the seal from Shufu, Seeckt will regret it. I'll make sure everyone in the motherland know that his temper is what prevented Germany from returning to prominence sooner."

Krause rubbed his brow and cocked his head to one side. "I thought the seal wasn't worth nearly as much as some collectors have suggested."

Wilhelm eyed Krause cautiously. "You want the truth?"

Krause nodded. "Of course."

"There's something we haven't told you about the seal. It's—"

Wilhelm stopped as he heard the creaking of a floorboard from down the hallway.

"They're already here," he whispered.

"I need to let the others know," Krause said.

Wilhelm shook his head. "It's too late for that now. Come on."

He led them to the balcony and wasted no time in climbing up on the railing and reaching for the ironwork surrounding the stoop just overhead. Wilhelm and Krause followed suit.

"There's no one in this room," Wilhelm said. "Get me that chair."

"You want a chair?" Krause asked. "They're going to have weapons."

"Get it now," Wilhelm said, pointing inside the room.

Krause smashed a pane of glass to release the deadbolt. Once he was inside, he grabbed a chair tucked neatly beneath a desk.

"What exactly are you going to do with this?" Krause asked.

"Just watch," Wilhelm said. "I trained these men. When

they're securing an area, they always check on the left first and then the right. They'll never see this coming."

Wilhelm removed his tie and threaded it through the back, enabling him to swing the chair back and forth.

"Ready?" Wilhelm asked. "Watch and learn."

Just as Wilhelm had predicted, the first soldier glanced to his left before turning back to the right. As he did, the chair crashed into his face, knocking him down.

"Dieter," cried another soldier who rushed out to check on his colleague.

The moment his head emerged from the doorway, he was smacked by Wilhelm's swinging chair.

"We've got to move now," Wilhelm said. "There will be more in a few minutes."

Wilhelm eased down to the balcony and removed all their weapons before shoving their bodies over the railing and onto the sidewalk several stories below.

"You think that was the best idea?" Reinhard asked. "Killing Seeckt's special revenge unit like that?"

"Knowing Seeckt, he's more likely to be impressed with that," Wilhelm said.

"There's still four more," Krause said.

Wilhelm checked the weapons and handed one to each man. He then unholstered his own gun and crept toward the door.

"There are two more in the hallway," Wilhelm whispered. "Let's draw them in before we kill these two."

Wilhelm motioned for Reinhard and Krause to hide behind an armchair in the corner. He took up a position on the other side of the room beneath the bed.

"Don't start shooting until I do," Wilhelm said.

After an agonizingly long minute, the door creaked as it slowly crept open.

Louis.

Wilhelm recognized one who he'd trained before the war. And now that same man was tasked with killing his mentor.

It's nothing personal.

Wilhelm took aim at Louis and his colleague's legs, firing several shots that made them instinctively reach for the pain. Reinhard and Krause squeezed off several rounds as well. The two attackers from the Schwarz unit collapsed on top of each other in a heap.

Wilhelm stood up. "Good work, gentlemen. Now we only have two more remaining."

The trio fanned out along the hotel's halls in search of the final two men. Wilhelm sneaked right up to one attacker and grabbed him from behind, slitting his throat. The final soldier was lurking in the hallway, trying to peek around the corner in Reinhard's direction. But Wilhelm watched as Krause head-butted the man, rendering him unconscious. Then Krause dragged his prize back to Wilhelm's room.

"Want to kill him too?" Krause asked.

Wilhelm shook his head. "No, I want to send Seeckt a message, something he's apparently wanting from us so badly."

Wilhelm removed his cigar trimmer and placed the soldier's thumb inside. With a strong squeeze, the blade ripped through the skin and all the way to the bone. The pain was intense enough that the man woke up. But Wilhelm wasn't done. He moved to the index finger and clipped it off as well.

"He'll never be able to shoot another weapon for the rest of his life," Wilhelm said proudly. He grabbed an envelope off the desk and dropped the bloody thumb and finger inside before sealing it up. The soldier was writhing in pain.

"Why? Why? Why? Just kill me," the man said.

"Come around again, and we can arrange for that, just like the rest of your colleagues here today," Wilhelm said. "In the meantime, return home and deliver this to Seeckt. Tell him that we're close to getting our hands on something really big and that we'll update him when we do."

Wilhelm ordered the rest of the unit to clean up the bodies and make them disappear. He didn't want to embarrass the Reichswehr, even if such an action would reflect poorly on Seeckt. Satisfied that no one would find out that they killed three men in the hotel—and that two more leaped to their deaths from above—Wilhelm crossed the street to pay Richard a visit.

When Wilhelm knocked, he didn't wait before storming inside. He was covered with blood and appeared disheveled.

"What happened to you?" Richard asked as he drew back.

"Any word yet?" Wilhelm asked.

"Nothing yet, but we still have—"

"Half an hour," Wilhelm said after glancing at this watch. "Okay, this better work. Understand?"

"I can't make him appear," Richard said.

"Well, you better figure out a way to make that happen because time's running out. And if it runs out for Shufu, it's going to run out for you too."

CHAPTER 22

Hangchow, China

HELEN SAT ON A PARK BENCH ACROSS THE STREET from Lu Shufu's house and waited for him to exit. The clock tower at the end of the street read 10:05 as a light cold rain fell. Tightening up the hood of her raincoat, Helen glanced down at the large envelope in her hand and wondered if the well-known antiquities dealer was going to leave as Shawn Lee claimed Shufu always did to play a game of cards after his wife went to bed.

The upstairs light went dim five minutes later, and two minutes after that, the front door opened. Shufu adjusted his hat and opened his umbrella. After surveying the quiet street, he turned to his right and walked at a brisk pace. He either didn't notice Helen or wasn't bothered with her presence since he never made eye contact.

Helen hustled to keep up with him, her heels clicking on the sidewalk. She attempted to tread more lightly, but it was virtually impossible. The rhythmic footfalls echoed off the nearby houses, eventually earning an over-the-shoulder glance from Shufu.

He stopped and waited for her to catch up to him. As she drew closer, he blurted out something in Chinese. When she didn't respond, he repeated himself. However, Helen remained silent until she got close enough for him to see her face.

"An American?" he asked in English.

She nodded. "I was wondering if I might be able to have a word with you."

"A married man walking late at night with a foreigner? That's a fine way to get some rumors started about you."

Helen cocked her head to one side and offered a faint smile. "Since when did you start caring about getting entangled in the rumor mill? If you were that concerned, I suppose you would've behaved differently in the past."

Shufu scowled and drew back. "What on earth are you talking about? And who are you?"

Helen handed the envelope to him and waited for him to open it and inspect the photos tucked inside. In a flash, his wide eyes narrowed as he ripped up the pictures and stuffed them into his pocket.

"I don't know who you think you are, but I will find out and I'll—"

"My name is Dorothy Dunning, and I'm working with your country's government."

"Why didn't my country send one of its own people?"

She shrugged. "I'm just a messenger for now, hopefully a courier, if you comply. But there are other people who will be involved to assure that you fulfill my request. I can assure you that you don't want to meet them."

"What's this all about?"

"Now that I've got your attention, your government has recently learned that you have come into possession of an important artifact that needs to be returned to its rightful owner."

He bristled at her demand. "I acquire everything legally. The government can't make any claim to any item that I purchase from another dealer."

"That only applies if the dealer you brokered the item

through holds a license. And since we already know how the people who sold you the item obtained it, we're aware that they don't have a license of any kind nor would they ever be granted one."

Shufu paced around, templing his fingers and touching them to his lips.

"This isn't a negotiation," Helen said. "If you don't hand over the item, those photos of you will be released publicly. And I'm quite certain you don't want to upset Governor Zhao, the man whose daughter you married."

"The governor is aware of this?" Shufu said as he scowled.

"Governor Zhao doesn't know anything about this—yet. But if pictures of you with another woman surfaced, your infidelity would surely anger him. And I doubt you would be granted a license to do business of any kind any more in this province—or any other province for that matter."

"Why not just make an attempt to seize the item?" Shufu asked.

"Apparently, someone at the Ministry of the Interior doesn't want to ruin your good name," Helen said. "Your expertise and relationship with foreign archeological societies have proven to be quite lucrative when it comes to selling licenses for digging."

Shufu sighed. "Okay, fine. I know what you want. Come with me."

Helen followed Shufu to his shop three blocks away. He looked around cautiously before unlocking the front door and entering. After they were both inside, he locked the door behind him.

"Just a precautionary measure," he said. "Obviously, word has traveled fast about this item."

"Wait right here."

Helen strolled around the floor, stopping to inspect the wide variety of offerings Shufu's store held. There were clay pots from ancient eras as well as an odd collection of money and guns used during the Civil War. In one corner of the room, a glass case displayed a Canadian beaver trap and a sketch of a flying machine attributed to the pen of Leonardo da Vinci. But a steel box with a small thick viewing portal housed his prized possessions—documents from a couple of Chinese dynasties more than eight hundred years old.

"Like what you see?" Shufu called from behind the closed door.

"Most of these things you see every day in America," she said.

He emerged from the back carrying a small black box. "I believe this is what you're after."

Ushering her over to the counter, he turned on a light and opened the lid to reveal the seal. The jade stone glinted as she rotated it beneath the lamp.

"I trust that this will satisfy your superiors, though I'm curious as to why they picked you to handle this task," he said, wrapping the seal with a small cloth and nestling it back inside the box. He snapped it shut before handing it to Helen.

"I already told you, I—"

"I know what you told me," Shufu said as he grabbed her wrist, "but now I want the truth. I want a name."

She ripped her hand away from his and glared at him. "I would suggest you address me more politely. Next time I might break all your fingers."

Shufu chuckled and pulled out a knife. "I know you aren't working with anyone in the Chinese government. So, I'm going to give you one more chance to tell me the truth."

He hunched over and held out his knife as he began circling her.

"Put that away before you make a very grave mistake," she said.

Before either of them moved again, a man wearing a black mask wrapped around his head stormed out of the back and rushed them both. Shufu spun toward the intruder and took a swipe at him with the knife. But the man evaded the slash and lunged straight for the box in Helen's hands. She jerked it back before he could get a solid grip on it. However, in the process, she got off-balance, which the man took full advantage of. He drove his shoulder into hers, sending her sprawling to the ground.

She looked up and saw the man hovering over her before he snatched away the box. Trying to regain her wits, she kicked at him, but he jumped out of the way, barreled over Shufu, and escaped through the back.

Shufu scrambled to his feet and started to run after the thief. Helen did likewise, racing past the antiquities dealer and reaching the backdoor first. Exploding into the alley, she wasn't prepared for the crowbar that met her square in the chest. Stunned by the blow, she staggered backward and hit her head on the wall as she fell unconscious.

CHAPTER 23

RICHARD RETURNED TO HIS BOOK, WHICH DIDN'T LAST long. While he found soothing the sound of the rain pelting the window, he could hardly concentrate given the angst he felt over whether or not Lu Shufu would show up. With only five minutes remaining until the imposed deadline, Richard wasn't sure what was going to happen. Getting up to stretch, Richard strode over to the window and peeked through the openings in the shade slats. In the hotel across the street, he could see Wilhelm and his men, one of which was gazing through a pair of binoculars at Richard before offering a friendly wave.

As Richard's impatience grew, he went to the door and cracked it. At the end of the hall, a man wearing a bellhop's uniform sat in a chair, rocked back on its two hind legs and leaning against the wall. He appeared disinterested, but Richard knew it was all an act. The man was one of the Reichswehr soldiers assigned to keep an eye on Richard in the event that there were any new developments.

Richard shut the door and returned to his pacing, checking his watch every few minutes. While Wilhelm seemed adamant about enforcing the deadline, Richard thought it was ridiculous, though he admitted to himself that it was a way to gauge if there was any interest in selling the artifact. Who would turn down ten million pounds? But it seemed unlikely that the Germans would dare to cart that much money with them around the world. In fact, Richard wondered why the Germans would even be on these expeditions if they owned that much money.

Ten million pounds would be more than enough to ignite some kind of conflict, maybe even sustain it for a few weeks to get their demands met. Or maybe they didn't even have the money at all. The notion that the Reichswehr was lying just to pique Shufu's interest scared Richard the most. With Shufu's ties to the Hong Kong pirates, Richard wondered just how many connections the antiquities dealer had to the underworld—and if he'd be vindictive to employ any of them to pursue Richard if the truth came out that there was no money.

Richard's handwringing came to an abrupt end when a knock on the door interrupted his spiraling thoughts. He turned to brace for Wilhelm storming inside and making good on his ultimatum but was pleasantly surprised when he only heard someone rapping on the door again.

Easing it open, he saw Shufu shaking out his umbrella and pooling water in the hall. Behind him, the Reichswehr agent sat upright and made eye contact with Richard.

"Come on in," Richard said, gesturing for Shufu to enter.

As Richard closed the door, the agent signaled for Richard to leave it unlocked. He nodded, acknowledging the order.

"So, I guess you've decided to sell," Richard said as he invited Shufu to sit in the chair in the corner of the room. "May I ask what made you change your mind?"

"Ten million pounds," Shufu said. "I'm a dealer, and I know a good deal when I see one. It's hard to turn down that large of a sum."

"That's all it took?"

Shufu straightened his tie. "That and fending off some would-be thieves at my shop tonight."

"Someone tried to steal to seal?"

He nodded. "I appreciate the civilized way your buyer is conducting his business. Fear and intimidation may get you what you want for now, but you will regret it."

"Speaking from experience?" Richard asked.

"Unfortunately, yes. But I've since changed my ways."

"So, did you bring the item?"

Shufu eyed Richard closely. "Did you bring the money?"

"My buyer is going to deliver it once I verify that you brought the seal."

"Are you some kind of expert?"

Richard shrugged. "Expert, specialist, connoisseur—call me whatever you like. I've been asked to verify the item's authenticity."

"And you've done this before on items dating back the ninth century?"

"Several times," Richard said followed by a sigh. "You either have the seal or you don't. I'd like to let my employer know whether or not he needs to deliver the money to this room."

"It's right here," Shufu said as he produced a small black box from his coat pocket.

Richard reached for it. "May I?"

"By all means."

Richard strode over to the table near the window and held it up, confident his silhouetted figure would set into motion the next part of Wilhelm's plan.

"It looks authentic to me," Richard said, "though I'd like to have a third party person verify it."

"Are they in the hotel?" Shufu asked.

"No, but—"

Shufu snatched the stone back. "Then our business for tonight has concluded."

"Wait, wait, wait," Richard said. "We can still work around this."

"Absolutely not. I know a rotten deal when I smell one."

Richard held his hands out in a gesture of surrender while backpedaling to impede Shufu's rush to get to the door. "I apologize for not having someone else here. My buyer tried to get another expert, but he couldn't make it tonight."

"There is no buyer," Shufu said as he reached into his pocket and snatched out a knife, flicking it open. "Now get out of my way before this gets any messier than it needs to be."

Richard turned aside to let Shufu pass. The dealer put his hand on the knob and turned it, glancing back over his shoulder at Richard.

"I almost didn't come because I knew this deal was too good to be true," Shufu said. "And I'm always disappointed when I don't trust my years of experience in this business."

"I guess you'll never know what's in that suitcase right there then," Richard said, pointing toward three pieces of luggage on the floor.

"It's not ten million pounds, I know that much," Shufu said as he turned to exit.

However, when he swung the door wide, three Reichswehr agent swarmed inside and pounced on him.

"Get off of me," Shufu said as he fought and clawed to get away from the agents.

Wilhelm strode into the room and found a spot against the wall where he watched like a casual observer.

"Help! Someone, please, help me!" Shufu said as he absorbed another body blow.

"Save your breath, Mr. Shufu," Wilhelm said. "There's no one listening—at least there's no one who's going to help you."

One more punch to Shufu's face knocked him unconscious.

"Where's the seal?" Wilhelm said as he knelt down next to Shufu's limp body.

"It was in a box in his coat pocket," Richard said reluctantly.

Wilhelm rooted around until he found the artifact, raising it triumphantly into the air.

"Finally, back where you belong," Wilhelm said before kissing the jade stone.

CHAPTER 24

Back in Wilhelm's hotel room, the German military commander celebrated with a glass of champagne and a cigar. He encouraged his men to revel in the moment, purchasing a dozen bottles for his troops to unwind with before embarking upon the next part of the mission. Richard took in the scene from a chair in the corner, wondering why the atmosphere had grown so festive.

"Why so glum?" Wilhelm joked as he tapped Richard with the butt of a bottle. "We are going to be worshipped as gods when we get back to Berlin. And if you help us find more treasure, you're going to have whatever you want."

Richard rubbed his forehead and looked at the ground, unresponsive to Wilhelm's comments.

"I'm talking to you," Wilhelm said. "Did you hear me? I said you could've—"

Richard held his hand up. "I heard you the first time. I'm sorry, but the prospect of doing things that strengthens the Reichswehr doesn't exactly ease my mind."

"Come off it, man," Wilhelm said, using his elbow to jab Richard. "You think you're better than us, don't you? You Americans are an arrogant bunch, always assuming that you stand on the moral high ground. Well, I tell you what, the next time I hear an American say—"

"Please stop," Richard said, holding up his hand. "I'm

not interested in your political posturing. You're celebrating as if you've won, yet you have no idea if you have the actual seal."

Wilhelm chuckled. "That's one of the reasons why I asked you to handle the negotiations with Shufu. He's going to be angry with you and come after you once he realizes what you've done."

"What I've done? Need I remind you that I was bowled over by your men just like he was. I feel like one of your soldiers gave me a little more than was necessary as he plowed through me to get to Shufu."

"There are always unintended consequences in battle."

"Is that what you think that was tonight? A battle? That was a simple robbery. You took something without paying for it."

Wilhelm sneered. "It didn't belong to him in the first place."

"Maybe, but it's not exactly like you can stake your claim as the original owner either. That seal has been around for more than a thousand years."

"And I'm fully within my right to claim it as my own."

Richard stroked his chin and eyed the artifact that Wilhelm was waving around flippantly.

"What is it?" Wilhelm asked.

"You can't rely upon me to verify the seal's authenticity. You need to get a third party to investigate it."

"What are you trying to say? That this is a fake?"

Richard shrugged. "Maybe. It looks real to me, but I'm not exactly an expert on Chinese antiquities."

"And who do I take this item to and trust that word isn't going to leak out that we have one of this country's greatest treasures?"

"I'm just suggesting that you might not want to plan

what you're going to say to your Kaiser in case this is indeed proven to be a replica."

Wilhelm huffed as he circled Richard's chair. "I know this is your first time seeing the seal up close, but I've held it in my hands before. I know what it feels like, what it smells like, even what it tastes like."

"You've licked the seal?" Richard asked, his eyes widening.

"This little stone represents my path back to respectability, maybe even prominence if General Seeckt admits that his attempt to eliminate my men was a failed one. I know what it feels like, every curve, every edge, every imprint. Right now, this is how I'm going to stay alive and stake my claim as one of the greatest leaders within the Reichswehr."

"You think Seeckt is going to heap praise upon you for finding something when he's already tried to kill you?"

"He'll have no choice."

Richard laughed. "You've definitely had too much of the bubbly if you think that. I've done enough research on power-hungry leaders to know that's not the case. He's going to take the seal from you and steal all the glory. You'll be left with nothing, not even a kind word about your efforts to obtain the seal. You'll be obliterated from the Germany military's history books if you're lucky, kept in them and viewed as a failure if not."

Wilhelm laughed and used the index finger hanging off his bottle to point at Richard. "You think you're going to get me upset about this, but you're not. Seeckt doesn't have that kind of power. And he'll have even less when I return so triumphantly to Berlin."

"If you go back without having that seal verified as authentic by a Chinese antiquities dealer, you might as well be signing your death certificate," Richard said. "They will kill you for acting as if you found a great treasure when all you found was a forgery that's utterly worthless."

"Very well then. We'll do it your way. First thing in the morning, I want you to set up an appointment with a local expert who can verify that this is indeed the heirloom seal of the realm."

"Of course," Richard said.

"And you'll always be in my sight," Wilhelm added. "So don't get any ideas that you'll be able to escape with it. My men will accompany you wherever you go."

"I wouldn't expect it to be any other way."

* * *

THE NEXT MORNING, Richard was escorted to a small shop three blocks away run by an aging gentleman named Shen Wong. According to the hotel concierge, Wong was not only Hangchow's residential expert on verifying ancient artifacts but also one of the most well known in the country. He worked with the museum in Peking to establish the age of some of China's oldest dynasty artifacts and had become highly sought-after when determining the worth of older items unearthed in the area by archeologists.

Wong was in the middle of sipping his tea when Richard entered the small shop. Officially, Wong repaired watches for a living, but his store was a mixture of watches and iron products. He also sold art supplies and proudly displayed several of his sketches on the walls.

"Mr. Wong," Richard said as he offered his hand while approaching the man. "I was hoping you could help me out."

Wong shook Richard's hand. "A pleasure to meet you. I wasn't aware of any digs occurring in the area. What brings you here this morning?"

Richard glanced over his shoulder at the two

Reichswehr guards standing near the doorway. "I have an item that was discovered elsewhere but recently acquired nearby."

"Must be something of great worth if you require two guards to escort you."

Richard shrugged. "That's precisely why we're here. We believe it to be an incredible find, but I need independent verification."

Richard dug into his pocket for the box containing the seal.

"What do you think I'll be looking at?" Wong asked as he placed his jeweler's glasses on and watched Richard carefully.

"The heirloom seal of the realm," Richard said.

Wong's eyes widened. "I've always wondered if I'd ever get to inspect such a rare find."

"Well, today just might be your lucky day," Richard said as he placed the box on the counter and opened the lid.

Wong slid his hand into a pair of white gloves before reaching for the seal. He carefully lifted it from the container and unwrapped the jade stone, his mouth falling agape as he did.

"This is incredible," he said. "A piece of history."

Wong's excitement was contagious. Richard shifted his weight from one foot to the other in anticipation of the result.

"So, can you verify that this is the heirloom seal of the realm?" Richard asked.

Wong remained silent as he studied the rock beneath a lamp, turning the artifact over and over in his hands.

Richard could hardly endure the tension, preparing to celebrate Wong's finding.

"Well?" Richard asked again.

Wong removed his glasses and placed the jade stone back into the box without wrapping it up. "Congratulations, you have yourself a fake."

"What?" Richard asked, his anticipation of joy morphing into anger. "How can that be? I thought this was—"

"Whoever gave this to you or sold this to you is an incredible good forger, probably skilled enough to fool most especially those unfamiliar with all the intricacies of dating stone. However, there is one telling characteristic. Come here."

Wong grabbed the seal and held it beneath the light. He handed Richard the jeweler's glasses and asked if he could see all the details in the stone. Richard nodded.

"This forger used nephrite, which is the type of jade used in ancient times in China," Wong explained. "However, the process by which they etched designs into this particular rock differed. See how it's smooth near the edges of the markings?"

"Yes. And that's bad?"

"No, it's just different than what things used to look like when they used a coarser surfaced to carve with. It should look more like this."

Wong handed Richard another seal carved out of jade. "This piece is over seven hundred years old and was created during the time when they still used the now-outdated process of carving. Do you see how the space around the marks aren't smooth but appear more like an orange peel?"

Richard nodded. "Yeah, I see it."

"That's what the seal should've looked like that you brought me if it was the lost heirloom seal of the realm. But what you have there is a very good fake. You might even be able to fool some people with that, though I'm not suggesting you dabble in such things, though apparently you already have."

Richard sighed. "Could you put this in writing for me so when I return this to my client that I won't get accused of being a thief or a liar?"

"Just give me a moment."

Richard paced around the room before walking over to the two Reichswehr guards. "It's a fake," he told them.

"A fake?" one of the guards repeated as he narrowed his eyes.

"Yes," Richard said. "Which one of you wants to deliver the bad news to Wilhelm? I'm sure he'll be delighted to hear this."

CHAPTER 25

HELEN SQUINTED AS SHE SLOWLY OPENED HER EYES. A damp cloth draped across her forehead leaked streaks of water down her cheeks. She scanned the room, unsure of where she was or how she got there. While she heard other conversations held in hushed tones, she couldn't see anyone due to the white curtain that encased the area around her bed.

I'm in a hospital. Why am I here?

She groaned as she sat up, her memory groggy from the previous night's events. As she reached for the glass of water on the bedside table, she was startled as a nurse invaded her private space.

"Don't try to do much," the woman said in a broken English accent. "You lay still. Understand?"

Helen nodded, but she didn't agree to the terms presented to her.

"Where am I?" Helen asked.

"St. Constantine's Hospital in Bangcchow."

"What day is it?" Helen asked.

"You don't know what day it is?" the nurse replied.

Helen shook her head. "I don't know how long I was out."

"Someone brought you here last night. You were a mess."

As she continued talking with the nurse, everything came back to Helen. The seal, the mission for Shawn Lee, the surprise attack at Shufu's shop, her betrayal of Richard. She almost wished none of it had come back so she could be one of those people she read about who forget everything about themselves and start over in life with a new identity. But she knew exactly who she was and why she was crammed into the hospital bed in a Catholic mission hospital. And she knew she had to get out as soon as possible.

Once the nurse left, Helen ripped off her gown, replacing it with the clothes she entered with. There were two large blood splotches, one on her side and the other near her knee. She lifted up the edge of her skirt and saw a large bandage affixed to her leg. Touching her side gingerly with the tips of her fingers, she winced at the pain, though she presumed the wound must have not been as deep since it wasn't bandaged. She grabbed her handbag, flinging it over her left shoulder before poking her head outside to see if there was anyone who would try to stop her. After determining that her escape would be of the nonchalant variety, she put on her coat and gritted through the pain in her leg to avoid drawing attention to her slight limp.

Helen exited the triage area and walked halfway down the hall before she locked eyes with Shawn Lee. Heavy lines marked his brow as he shook his head slowly.

"I'm so sorry, Helen," he said. "I only left your side for a few minutes, and I was just coming back to check on you."

He reached for her shoulder, which she withdrew and kept walking past him.

"I swear, I had no idea that you would be in so much danger, I—"

Helen spun and stamped her foot. "You had no idea? You expect me to believe that?" She glanced up and down the corridor before continuing in a hushed tone. "You directed me to threaten him in order to get that seal," she said. "I was more than aware of the danger I would be facing. So, don't come down here and try to patronize me and act as if you didn't understand the inherent risks associated with such a ploy."

"I'm not lying. You have to believe me. I never thought—"

Helen glared at him. "I have some things to do and think about before we speak again."

"I have something else for you to do and it's really critical that I have your help this time," Lee said, his eyes pleading as he spoke.

She turned her back and strode down the hallway. "I'll think about it."

Helen marched out of the hospital. She was so angry, she barely noticed any pain in her leg. Once out on the street, she sought a place to send a telegram to Hank Foster. While she wasn't likely to reach him soon, she at least wanted to update him with what had transpired on the mission thus far. And none of it was good.

After a few minutes, she found a bank where she could send a note. She comprised the following message:

> IN HANGCHOW. RICHARD CAPTURED.
> WORKING WITH LEE TO GET SEAL BEFORE
> GERMANS. WILL UPDATE LATER.

She re-read the note and sighed. It was vague but that's how telegrams worked. No space to fill in all the details. Just cold facts dished out as quickly as possible. The luxury of providing any context was lost in the clipped format. But if Foster felt so inclined to look for them or send some help, at least he knew where they would be.

After she sent the message, she decided to stroll past

Shufu's shop, something she knew was against her better judgment. Remaining on the opposite side of the street, she cast quick glances toward the storefront to see if she could determine if any activity was taking place inside. She circled the block three times and hadn't seen the slightest sign that the business was open, but that changed the fourth time around.

As she walked past, a man exited and was followed outside by Shufu. Helen had to restrain herself from sprinting across the street and demanding answers. She would find another time, and she would fulfill Shawn Lee's promise herself if she didn't leave with the seal.

Two blocks later, someone bumped her from behind, knocking her off her stride. She scowled as she turned to see who the perpetrator was.

"Pardon me, ma'am," Shawn Lee said, tipping his hat. "I'm sorry. I know you're upset with me, but I just had to apologize again for how things went down last night. An attack like that was the last thing I expected. It was cold and calculated on his part. He obviously doesn't think I'll use the photos to extort him."

"The photos you lost last night?" Lee asked.

"You don't have any other copies?"

"Of course we do, and here they are," he said, handing her a packet of them. "Go to his shop now and hand these to him. This needs to be done during the day while his shop is open so nothing happens again like what happened last night. Think you can do that for us?"

She shrugged. "I guess so, though I'd really like to punch him in the face after what he pulled last night."

"Just make the exchange. I have some men who will be outside in case he tries anything again."

"Right now?" Helen asked.

He nodded. "Go. It'll be better this way."

Helen looked over Lee's shoulder and saw three men standing half a block away, trying to act casual. But she identified them right away as Lee's men.

"I thought you said I wouldn't have any support," she said.

"Them?" Lee said, looking behind him. "Given what happened last night, I thought it might be best to hire a few men for reinforcement, just in case."

"Tell them to keep up," she said.

Helen spun on her heels and walked two blocks back to Shufu's shop. His eyes widened and his mouth dropped when she entered.

"Are you okay?" Shufu said. "I really felt bad about what happened last night. And I just—"

"You pulled a knife on me," she said. "It's hard for me to believe you actually care about my well being."

"I know," Shufu said. "I was caught off guard and wasn't myself."

"You know what I hate more than anything?" Helen said as she marched straight toward him. "It's a liar. Just stop it. I know you orchestrated that attack last night as if it was some robbery attempt. But I know better."

"That's not what happened at all. It was—"

"Enough," she said, the edge in her voice growing with each passing second. "You got the photos. Do you even have the seal?"

"I'm almost too embarrassed to admit this, but the one I showed you last night was a fake."

"So the thieves didn't take the original?"

Shufu shook his head. "I'll let you see it later tonight in exchange for that packet of photos in your hand and the negatives later this evening. Do we have a deal?"

"Let me see it," Helen said. "I need to know I'm not walking into another one of your traps."

Shufu sighed. "I'm not sure that's something I want to do with your henchman right outside."

"They won't come in unless I summon them," she said.

"Fine, I'll show it to you right now."

Shufu ambled behind the counter and over to a safe before opening it. He returned to the display case near Helen and clicked on a light.

"Here it is," he said. "The real thing."

Helen gasped as she peered through a magnifying glass to study the ancient seal. It appeared just like the one Shufu had shown her the night before only more weathered, like something she would expect from an artifact that had been lost for almost a millennium.

"I'll be back tonight at seven o'clock to make the exchange," she said. "And you better make sure no one else is here."

"You do the same," he said with a snarl.

Helen pushed open the door and felt a blast of cold wind hit her as she strode back onto the sidewalk. She was ready to end this mission once and for all and do the thing she wanted the most—find Richard.

* * *

LU SHUFU SITUATED THE PAPER in front of him before dipping his pen into a well of ink. Less than twenty-four hours earlier, he wielded a knife in an attempt to find out who was trying to steal the seal of the realm and had failed. But all he needed to do was give the local delivery boy a couple of fens to go the hospital and follow Dorothy Dunning around. He came back with a description of the man she appeared to be working with—and Shufu knew right away who he was dealing with.

Upon learning the man's identity, Shufu hatched a scheme, one in which he would be able to eliminate a man he detested and direct the thieves' attention elsewhere. The attack on his store the night before underscored how urgent it was to utilize the seal. He was a big target while in possession of a precious object that people would do anything to get their hands on. And he wasn't excited about the prospect of it costing him his life. Such danger would soon disappear once he posted the letter to Governor Zhao.

What good was being the governor's son-in-law if I don't take advantage of it?

Shufu finished writing and walked outside. He whistled at the young spy on the other side of the street and signaled to cross over. Shufu instructed the lad to hand-deliver the letter to Governor Zhao's residence right away and then gave him a package to deliver to a local hotel.

CHAPTER 26

HELEN RETURNED TO SHUFU'S SHOP THAT EVENING
with the negatives stuffed into an envelope. She
knocked on the door and waited for him to unlock
it. Without any interior lights on, she started to wonder if he
was even there. She rapped on the glass once more and
pressed her face up against the window to see if she could
tell if anyone was inside. A few moments later, the door
opened, and Shufu gestured for her to enter without saying
a word.

Once they were inside, he locked the door behind them.

"Wait here," he said. "I want to check the back exit
again to make sure what happened last time doesn't happen
again."

Helen drummed her fingers on a display case to combat
the boredom. She scanned the room for any potential objects
she could utilize as weapons should another ambush ensue.

When Shufu returned, he was carrying a small box and
placed it on the counter in front of her.

"The negatives," he said, holding out his hand.

"Let me see the seal first," she said.

Shufu lifted the lid to reveal the seal. "There it is, in all
its glory."

Helen gazed at the green gem before reaching to pick
it up. Shufu abruptly placed his hand over it.

"The negatives," he said.

She handed him the package containing the film and watched as he studied each frame intently beneath a magnifying glass and a light. Helen drummed her fingers on the counter as his inspection dragged on.

"Satisfied?" Helen asked after a couple of minutes.

He looked up and eyed her closely. "Do you have somewhere to be? And quite frankly I don't care if you do or not. I'm not just going to hand over the greatest artifact to ever come through those doors without making sure I'm getting what I'm trading for."

"I hope your indiscretion was worth it," she said.

"I can assure you that it'll never be worth it based on the price I could fetch for the seal."

"A costly lesson," she said with a hint of a smile.

When Shufu placed his magnifying glass down, he looked up at Helen before glancing back at the seal. "She's all yours."

Helen conducted a more thorough inspection for a few seconds, studying the contours and smooth lines around the ancient stone.

"Satisfied?" Shufu asked.

She placed the seal back into the box and stuffed it into her pocket. "I think this concludes our business."

Shufu walked her to the door and unlocked it, pausing before opening it. "Tell your government friend I hope I never see him again."

"I'll be sure to pass along the message."

Helen hustled along the sidewalk until she reached the corner where two of Lee's hired guards helped escort her back to the boat where Lee was waiting.

"Did you get it?" Lee asked, offering his hand to help Helen as she stepped aboard.

She nodded and patted her coat pocket. Lee's face lit up with a wide grin.

"No knives or ambush this time?" he asked.

"It was smooth. Almost too smooth, though Shufu took forever to verify the authenticity of the negatives."

He gestured for her proceed ahead of him toward the dining hall. "The thing about someone like Shufu is that he gave up the seal, but it's not like we won't be able to gather more evidence of other indiscretions whenever we want. That man is a master at making a mess of his life. The fact that he's still married to Governor Zhao's daughter is one of the biggest mysteries on this planet."

"Enough about Shufu," Helen said. "I'm sure you want to see this, and I'll get out of your hair so I can find my colleague."

"Of course," Lee said.

He took a seat at one of the tables across from Helen and stared with wide eyes as she revealed the stone. It only took a few seconds of studying the artifact up close to realize the painful truth: Shufu gave Helen a fake.

"What is this?" Lee said as he slammed down his fist. "What kind of fool do you think I am?"

Helen drew back, unsure of what to make of Lee's sudden outburst.

"This is the one he gave me, I swear," she said

Lee snapped his fingers and pointed at Helen before instructing his men to search her. The two men who minutes earlier had been escorting her to the boat and protecting her from any potential danger were now rifling through her pockets and ripping off her coat in search of the seal.

"Let go of me," Helen said. "I don't have any other seal. That's the one Shufu gave me."

Lee stood and stamped his foot. "I don't believe you.

196 | GARRETT DRAKE

Shufu is a skilled forger, but he would never try to pass this off as the real thing."

"Maybe he's slipping because this is what he gave me. Or maybe he thought that he could get away with it since hardly anyone had held the actual stone," Helen said, growing bolder with each statement. "Besides, what makes you an expert on an artifact you've never seen?"

Lee narrowed his eyes and seethed for a few seconds before he started pacing around the room. "I'll tell you what. I'll give you one chance to prove to me that you're not lying before I kill you."

"Kill me?" Helen asked. "I thought we were working together, like as a partnership. I scratch your back, you scratch mine. You help me get to Hangchow so I can find my colleague on my own in exchange for retrieving an item for you through extortion. Now you're targeting me."

"Anyone who holds that seal will draw my ire. It doesn't belong to them. It belongs to the people of China."

"How about I leave now and we just consider this the end of our arrangement?" she said as she headed toward the door.

Two of Lee's guards shuffled in front of the doorway, effectively blocking it. Helen spun around and locked eyes with Lee.

"This is not acceptable," she said. "Tell those men to move now, or I'll be quite forthcoming in all the details about this incident when I speak with Hank next."

"No, that's not how this is going to work," Lee said. "You don't get to dictate the terms of this situation, especially since you were the one who freely handed over my only leverage for this garbage."

Lee picked up the forged seal and hurled it downward. Upon impact with the floor, the rock splintered into scores of pieces.

"What you're going to do is go back down to Shufu's place tonight and steal the real seal of the realm and bring it back to me," Lee said. "My men waiting outside will accompany you. And if you don't bring it back to me, I'll make sure the only place you'll be able to reunite with your colleague will be in the afterlife. Understand?"

Helen nodded.

"Go," Lee said as he pointed toward the door.

Helen ignored him, darting toward the gun on the table. "I need protection," she said as she stuffed it into her purse.

"Just go," Lee said with a growl.

* * *

HELEN TOOK UP A POSITION on a rooftop across the street from Shufu's shop and peered through a pair of binoculars. As far as she could tell, all the lights were out, and Shufu appeared to have gone home for the evening. She waited another half hour just to be sure before climbing down and making her attempt to break inside.

The back door was locked, but there were a series of small windows running about twelve feet off the ground along the side of the building. She glanced around to make sure no one was watching. Lee's henchmen were the only people in sight.

How did I not recognize this?

Muttering beneath her breath, she berated herself for not being able to see through Lee's generous offers. He'd been using her like a pawn, and she fell for it.

The brick provided sufficient enough footholds for her to scramble up the side of the wall and open the window. She was able to contort her body enough to slither inside. Once her feet hit the floor, she scanned the warehouse, which was almost completely dark. A few stray rays of moonbeams illuminated the area just enough for her to find the light switch on the far wall.

Helen crept toward a workbench, which was stacked with replicas of the seal of the realm, all resembling the one Shufu had given her a few hours earlier.

How do I know which one is the real thing?

She searched around for anything that looked slightly different, a little more worn. But she didn't see anything.

The safe.

Helen remembered Shufu's safe in the front of the store she'd seen him access before. She stole across the floor and knelt down behind the counter next to the large safe. Placing her ear against the door, she started to turn the knob until she heard a click. In less than a minute, she'd managed to get it open. However, when she did, she didn't see anything close to the jade stone.

"Where is it?" she whispered to herself.

The safe door moved suddenly, resulting in Helen losing her balance. She scrambled back to her feet and was eye to eye with Shufu.

"Looking for this?" he said as he held up the seal.

Helen grabbed for it but was greeted with a knee into her chest. She doubled over in pain and was promptly seized by a pair of men who escorted her to the back of the warehouse.

"You're going to pay for this," she said.

Shufu chuckled. "I'm not the one who broke into this store. That was you. And have you heard what we do to thieves here in China?"

She glared at him, her nostrils flaring.

"Well, trust me. It's not pleasant. Have a nice life, Dorothy, or whatever your name is."

The guards secured her to a chair in the back and retreated inside a small office. Helen wrestled with the bindings for a couple of minutes before realizing she'd been tied up well and wasn't going to get anywhere for a while.

Inside the office, the men held a loud conversation in Chinese. However, Helen was adept at understanding the language and listened intently. After a few minutes of eavesdropping, her anger toward Shufu grew as he talked about selling multiple seals to different museums around the world. Then she furrowed her brow.

"Tomorrow, we'll be rid of the person who's been tormenting me from almost the second I got my hands on the seal of the realm," Shufu said. "And then we'll get down to the business of using the stone for its true purpose."

True purpose? What have they not been telling me about the seal?

CHAPTER 27

RICHARD CROUCHED LOW AGAINST THE SIDE OF THE wall behind Reinhard and waited for Wilhelm's orders. In the time that had passed since Shufu sold Wilhelm a fake seal, the Reichswehr had been scheming the way to storm the antiquities dealer's store. With the soldiers in place and ready to execute their plan, Wilhelm glanced around one final time to check if everyone was where they were supposed to be.

"Don't get any ideas," Wilhelm said as he eyed Richard. "If I see you trying to make a run for it, I'll shoot you myself."

"Damned if I do, damned if I don't," Richard said with a shrug.

"If you survive this raid, then you'll at least have a chance with me," Wilhelm countered. "That's the only hope you've got. So I suggest you stay close and avoid getting into trouble."

"You could've left me at the hotel," Richard said.

"And wasted one of my men watching you? Not a chance. We need everyone we've got."

"But if you truly want my help now, I suggest you let me have a weapon," Richard said. "I've become a pretty good marksman as of late."

Wilhelm huffed a soft laugh through his nose and ignored Richard.

"On my signal, men," Wilhelm said. There was a brief pause before he said, "now!"

The men crashed into the door and had it open before Richard could count to five. And while that was the goal Wilhelm had stated earlier that he was aiming for, it was still five seconds that Shufu and his men would have to scramble into place before the ambush began in earnest. Richard was unsure any of it would work, which is why he didn't mind staying with Reinhard during the raid. The farther away out of the line of fire, the better as far as Richard was concerned.

The plan was simple in its conception. However, the degree of difficulty was rather high as it consisted of Shufu relinquishing the location of the authentic seal of the realm. Richard had seen firsthand how persuasive Wilhelm could be and wondered if his methods would produce the desired results.

As soon as the doors were battered down, the Reichswehr troops broke up into two groups. They took up positions on opposite sides of the warehouse and trained their weapons on the office. The only sign of occupancy was the yellow glow of a lamp leaking from beneath the crack between the door and the floor. Although Wilhelm would've preferred to unleash a hail of bullets on Shufu, the German commander needed the store owner alive.

"Mr. Shufu, we know you're in there," Wilhelm said. "We don't want to hurt you, but we do want some answers."

Shufu opened the door and hurled a grenade into the middle of the warehouse area. At the same time, men stationed atop the two small offices in the cavernous room opened fire on the Reichswehr. And had the Reichswehr not been able to seek cover so quickly, it could've turned into a blood bath. Instead, it was more of a standoff.

Weaponless, Richard curled up in a fetal position and

hid behind one of the shelves. Bullets peppered the wall nearby, but he was confident he'd managed to find a spot that was out of the direct line of fire. It was hard for him to tell if one side was starting to gain an advantage with only the pale moonlight to illuminate the room. He wanted to fight back if only to give himself a fair shot at surviving.

Meanwhile, Reinhard appeared focused and intense as he fired away at the two different clusters of shooters.

After about two minutes, there was a lull in the gunfire. The only sounds Richard heard were casings getting kicked across the floor and guns reloading until he heard a familiar voice. More like a scream—a woman's scream.

Richard craned his neck around the edge of the bookshelf and saw Helen tied up at the far end of the building just outside an office. And that was all he needed to see. He sprang to his feet and sprinted toward her.

Right at that moment, the two sides re-engaged. And both sides seemed uninterested in Richard, who clearly had no weapon.

He raced up to Helen and untied her.

"Am I glad to see you," she said. "Though this isn't how I pictured our reunion."

"That makes two of us."

"I didn't think I'd live to see the morning," she said.

"We're not out of here yet."

Richard worked furiously on her hands. Once they were free, they each went to work on her legs, loosening the knots the rope fell limp on the ground. She noticed her purse lying nearby and raced over to grab it before returning to Richard.

He grabbed her hand. "Ready to make a run for it?"

"Whenever you are."

He let go of her hand as they both leaped to their feet and sprinted toward the closest exit at the far back corner of the room.

Richard was about ten meters away from the door when he glanced over his shoulder, just in time to see Wilhelm train his gun on him.

"Halliburton!" Wilhelm's face was filled with rage as he shouted.

Richard wasn't sure he could avoid a bullet from Wilhelm so he did the only thing he could, darting sharply to the right to draw the German's fire away from Helen.

Wilhelm shouted something, this time in German, and fired his weapon.

Richard fell to the ground.

CHAPTER 28

IF REINHARD WAS BEING HONEST WITH HIMSELF, HE KNEW Richard had slipped away. But making sure the captive stayed with him was a Wilhelm obsession, marked by greed. Wilhelm craved power, and if he was the one who returned to Berlin with enough money to restart the German military and help the country regain respectability globally, he acted as if he might ascend to the leader of the entire Reichswehr. It was a notion that made Reinhard laugh.

While Reinhard was fiercely loyal to his country, he still hadn't buried his wife or been there to console his children. He knew what he signed up for when he pledged to defend the motherland, he just didn't think the Reichswehr policies would be so cruel.

So when Richard escaped from underneath his nose, Reinhard shrugged it off, staying focused on the main mission of getting the seal of the realm. Ultimately, it was the fastest way for him to get back home.

And when he saw Wilhelm's preoccupation with Richard, Reinhard had to do something drastic. In this case, it was tackling his commander to the ground.

The veins in Wilhelm's neck protruded as he prepared to fire at Richard. But Reinhard put his shoulder into the side of Wilhelm's ribcage, ruining his aim and sending him sprawling across the floor. To sell the act as one of heroism rather than sabotage, Reinhard laid on top of Wilhelm for a couple of seconds, firing at the combatants in the upper corner of the room.

The two scrambled for cover and remained there for a moment.

"What were you doing?" Wilhelm demanded.

"Saving your life," Reinhard said. "The sniper up there had you dead in his sights. He would've killed you if you stayed upright any longer."

"But Halliburton, he—"

"Forget about him," Reinhard said. "The seal is in this place somewhere, and we're not leaving until we have it."

Wilhelm cracked a faint smile and grabbed Reinhard's face. "This is the reason you're my second in command. Now let's take these men out."

The battle raged on for another fifteen minutes. One by one, the Reichswehr picked off the shooters, turning the battle in their favor. In the end, there was only one gunman left. He laid down his weapon and held up his hands in surrender. Wilhelm shot him anyway.

"Find Shufu and bring me that seal," Wilhelm ordered.

The Reichswehr agents spread out around the room, tearing through everything from the office to the shelves housing all of Shufu's precious artifacts. They even cracked the safe but found nothing but stacks of money.

Reinhard sifted through Shufu's files but didn't find anything of note pertaining to the seal. There were a few old maps, outlining archeological digs he'd likely participated in or was tracking. But when it came to any information that could lead them to the Shufu's next destination, Reinhard was coming up empty.

"Please tell me you've found something, anything," Wilhelm said.

Reinhard shook his head. "You?"

Wilhelm held up a fistful of replica seals. "Look what this thief was doing. He was making fake seals and probably would've tried to fool others like he fooled us."

"I'm sure he wasn't concerned with the consequences of his business ethics."

"Regardless of what he was up to, we need to find him or figure out where he was going before he disappears and we have to go back to Berlin empty-handed, something I'm not fond of doing."

"We may have to if we don't find that seal because I understand our treasury is almost empty."

"Not anymore," Wilhelm said, holding up a stack of pounds. "We found about ten thousand pounds inside the safe. That should hold us over until we get back to Berlin."

"And then some," Reinhard said.

Wilhelm shrugged. "Maybe, but if we don't succeed here, we'll have to make a detour to Japan. I just learned about something else we might be able to retrieve there."

"With all due respect, sir, I haven't even—"

Wilhelm held up his hand. "This is about duty and honor."

"And your fear of going back to Berlin without any of the treasures you promised to deliver."

Wilhelm bristled. "And you aren't afraid? I wouldn't be surprised if they lined us up and shot us all."

"That'd be lunacy and you know it."

"General Seeckt hates us. Just know that you were warned. Now, I'll be back in five minutes for an update. Keep looking."

Reinhard noticed a bottle of rum sitting on a bookshelf behind Shufu's desk. It was almost as if the liquor beckoned him.

Well, I could use a drink.

Reinhard picked up the bottle to inspect it when he noticed a slight indentation in the wood comprising the back wall of the bookshelf. He reached out and touched it, and the floor began to move and rotate. A few seconds later, Reinhard was standing in another room.

Maps and other posters decorated the drab gray stonewalls. However, they weren't random. There were certain cities circled. Then Reinhard noticed the titles stripped across the top of each map. He read each one, unfamiliar with the names until he came to "The Seal of the Realm."

There you are.

He walked up to it and studied the route outlined on the paper, starting in Hangchow and ending next to a city that had a star etched next to it.

Now we know where you're going, Mr. Shufu. And we'll be ready for you.

"I found something," Reinhard shouted.

A few seconds later, Wilhelm joined him in the room. "Would you look at that?"

Reinhard turned toward one of the other soldiers who'd just strode into the room. "We need tickets for the first train heading east in the morning."

"Where are we going?" he asked.

Wilhelm stroked his chin and smiled. "We're going to Mukden—and we'll leave there with the treasure."

CHAPTER 29

RICHARD HIT THE GROUND AND ROLLED A COUPLE OF times before skidding to a stop. He looked back to see Reinhard tackling Wilhelm, enabling Richard to avoid getting shot. Richard scrambled to his feet before dashing through the door and into the street where Helen was waiting.

Before he could say a word, she grabbed his face and pulled it close. Then she planted a kiss on his lips. Richard was stunned by her forward move.

"I'm sorry," she said. "I didn't—just don't take that the wrong way."

"I'm not sure there's any other way to take it," Richard said.

"Never mind. Just pretend it didn't happen."

"We need to get out of here before this fight spills out into the street," he said. "Follow me."

They walked swiftly for a couple of blocks before stopping in an alley.

"Are you all right?" she asked.

Richard felt his chest and arms then glanced at his legs. "I'm fine. And you?"

"I'd be better if I had the seal," she said.

He was pleased to return his focus to the task at hand. "Is it still in there?"

"Maybe, though I'm inclined to think it's where Shufu is—and I don't think he's in there anymore."

"What are you even doing here?" he asked. "I mean, how did you even find me?"

"Look, I'm really sorry about what I did back on Lantau Island. I didn't think through everything, which is a problem I sometimes have."

"It's all right," Richard said with a dismissive wave. "I'm still in one piece. And you're in one piece. And—"

"We don't have the seal."

"I figured out that much since I hadn't seen you anywhere near the precious stone since we arrived here," Richard said.

"But here I am tonight."

"How did you get tangled up in all this mess?"

Helen sighed. "It's a long story that I'll tell you soon enough, but right now we need to find Shufu."

"I hope you've got some ideas about where he could be because I've been in the dark the past few days," Richard said. "Wilhelm had me serving as some kind of broker to buy the seal, but it was a setup."

"So you met Shufu?"

"A couple of times briefly. He was an interesting fellow."

"Well, he tied me up and tried to kill me," Helen said. "So, I'd use a different adjective to describe him than interesting."

"Do you have any idea about where he might go if he's hiding out with the seal?"

"That's a good question," she said. "Tonight before all hell broke loose I heard Shufu talking with several other men about the seal's true purpose. It made me wonder if I was in the dark about why everyone wanted this seal so badly. I just assumed that they were wanting to profit off of it by selling it, but I think there might be more to it."

"If there was talk of that among the Reichswehr, I never heard it. So, your guess is as good as mine."

"I don't even have a guess at this point."

"Where are you staying?" Richard asked.

"I'm at a hotel a few blocks from here. We can go back there and regroup."

"Will you be at risk?"

"Maybe, but I'll ask to switch rooms and pay the hotel staff to keep quiet. It'll at least buy us a good night's sleep before we figure out what to do next."

Helen led Richard back to her hotel. Aside from a couple of guests sitting around reading newspapers in the lobby, it was barren.

"At least Mr. Lee isn't here," she said.

"Is that who brought you to Hangchow?"

She nodded. "I thought he was a government agent, but I'm realizing he was someone else."

Helen slipped the man at the counter some extra money to move her to another room and ordered him not to tell anyone where.

"Of course, madam," the man said as he slipped the money into his coat pocket.

Richard followed Helen upstairs where they both collapsed into the two armchairs in the room. He unloosened his tie and remained still for a few minutes without saying a word while Helen disappeared into the bathroom.

When she emerged, her hair was up in a bun, and she was wearing a robe provided by the hotel.

"I appreciate you taking the risk that you did tonight," she said. "If you hadn't, I might be—"

"Ssshhh," Richard said, placing his index finger to his

lips. "Let's not think about what could've been. I've found that's a dangerous place to go sometimes."

"We need to leave first thing in the morning," she said. "I'm positive that Mr. Shawn Lee will come after me since I failed to deliver what I promised."

"You were supposed to give him the seal?"

She nodded. "And I'm not even sure he's any better than the man who tried to kill me. I just know he certainly doesn't work for the Chinese government like he first claimed."

"I'll sleep with one eye open on the couch," he said. "If he tries anything, I'll be ready."

"I'd appreciate that," she said. "I could use a good night's sleep."

Just as Helen eased under the cover, someone slipped a note beneath the door.

"What's that?" she asked as she sat up in bed.

Richard strode over to the door and collected the note.

"What's it say?" Helen asked.

"Meet me in the lobby tomorrow morning at 8 o'clock. We need to talk," Richard read aloud. "Think we should go?"

Helen climbed out of bed and walked over to her purse sitting on the floor nearby. "Why don't you go, but take protection."

She rooted around in her purse for a moment before producing a gun then handed it to Richard.

"You're going to need this in the morning," she said.

"If I don't come back in a timely manner, you might want to consider an escape plan."

She nodded and turned off the bedside lamp. "Good luck."

CHAPTER 30

BEFORE RICHARD FELL ASLEEP, HE SPENT AT LEAST AN hour mulling over in his mind who would want to meet with them. And there were hardly any possibilities that made it easy for Richard to relax. Reichswehr troops? Wilhelm? Reinhard? Shufu? Hank Foster? And those were just the names of the first few people who popped into his head. Richard also couldn't rule out that it was someone else. But why so secretive? He threw his coat over his right hand to shroud the fact that he was holding a gun.

Morning sunlight streamed through the windows as Richard reached the lobby, he glanced around until he noticed a man sitting in the far corner reading a book. His face was in the shadows from the brim of his hat, but his silhouette looked familiar to Richard. As he drew near, he was sure who had summoned him.

Ashenden.

Richard stole across the room and took a seat next to the British spy.

"Sorry about my note being so vague," Ashenden said. "You can never be too careful in China."

"That's some sage advice I wished I'd received earlier," Richard said.

"Having the time of your life here?" Ashenden asked. "Everything you imagined and more?"

"Quite frankly, I'll just be content to escape with my life once I leave this place."

"A noble goal, though if you are willing to help me, I'm sure the odds of achieving it will diminish considerably."

"What exactly are you doing here?" Richard asked.

"I suppose it's all your fault," Ashenden said.

"My fault?"

"You did help me successfully retrieve that decoder, which is why I was reassigned so quickly to China. If I'd spent another few days chasing the Japanese spy, I'd likely be somewhere else in the world. But since I was so close to China at a time my government needed me here, I was the best candidate for the assignment."

"And what kind of assignment is that?"

"Stopping the Germans, of course," Ashenden said.

Richard nodded. "The more, the merrier, I suppose."

"Not necessarily, but in this case, it might actually be helpful. I often find that too many cooks in the kitchen don't always lead to the meal everyone hoped for. But this time . . ."

"What prompted you to come here?" Richard asked in a hushed tone as he edged forward in his seat.

"I asked around if anyone had seen an American woman in the past few days," he said. "Your colleague stands out far more in a place like this than a man does."

"Clever. And you assumed I'd just be with her?"

"I wasn't wrong, was I?" Ashenden asked. "Something didn't happen, did it?"

"It's been quite the adventure, but I'm somehow still here."

"And your partner?"

"She's here too. Perhaps we should make our way upstairs so she can hear all this too. Plus, it'd be prudent to be more discreet."

"Lead the way," Ashenden said.

They returned to Helen's room and got reacquainted briefly before Ashenden continued explaining why he was in China.

"British intelligence intercepted a message from the German military that originated in China," Ashenden said.

"Saying what exactly?" Helen asked.

Ashenden glanced around the room. He leaned in close and answered in a hushed tone. "One member of the Reichswehr unit sent a telegram to General Seeckt informing him that they almost had their hands on the seal and that he needed to send a ship to help bring back the treasure."

"A ship?" Richard asked with a furrowed brow. "That seal easily fits in your pocket."

Ashenden nodded. "Precisely what I thought when I first learned this bit of news. However, there is a little known legend that suggests the seal wasn't so sought after because of its alleged divine stamp on an emperor's decree. It's actually a key to an enormous treasure."

"This kind of story is always popular," Helen said. "How could this be kept a secret?"

Ashenden shrugged. "It's one of those tales that most archeologists haven't given much credence to, suggesting that it's sheer fantasy."

"But not all archeologists?" Richard asked.

"That's right," Ashenden said. "England's own Dr. Thurston Miller held a different theory, one we learned about when we recovered some of his stolen diaries six months ago in Africa."

"So where is this treasure supposedly hidden?" Helen asked.

Ashenden shook his head. "No one knows for sure. And the few archeologists who were brave enough to go against the prevailing thought that the seal of the realm is just a seal didn't offer up many theories about the location of the treasure."

Richard held up his index finger. "Except for Dr. Miller."

"Except for Dr. Miller," Ashenden repeated. "In fact, he was very specific about where he thought the riches were housed, even though he only performed one dig in China. He promised that he'd return one day, but someone made sure that he didn't."

"And where did Dr. Miller think the treasure was stored?" Helen asked.

"Somewhere in the Great Wall of China near Mukden," Ashenden said. "In fact, he left very specific instructions on how to reach the precise point containing the port leading to the fortune."

"This is all well and good," Richard said. "But we don't even know who has the seal."

Ashenden scowled. "What do you mean?"

"What he means is that earlier tonight we witnessed a shootout between a local antiquities dealer—"

"Lu Shufu?" Ashenden asked.

She nodded. "You know him?"

"I've had a run-in with him before."

Helen continued. "Shufu and his men were in a gunfight with the Reichswehr."

"And you just left without the seal?"

"It was a little more complicated than that," Richard said. "Shufu was holding Helen captive, while I was a prisoner of the Reichswehr."

"Yet you both managed to escape? Impressive. Well, I must hear more about that on the way in the morning."

"Where are we going when we don't know where the seal is?" Helen asked.

Ashenden winked. "To Mukden, of course. There's a train that leaves this afternoon heading east. Whoever ended up with the seal is going after that treasure."

CHAPTER 31

THE TRAIN CLICKED ALONG THE TRACKS THROUGH THE darkness as Wilhelm sat in the dining car and stared at the dregs from his glass of brandy. It was a little early to be drinking, but he didn't care. He drained what was left and slid the tumbler down the counter toward the bartender. Checking his watch, he contemplated going to bed but decided he needed one more drink.

"Another, sir?" the man asked.

Wilhelm didn't look up, managing little more than a nod and a grunt. He was still fuming over his failure to regain possession of the seal of the realm. If he didn't return to Berlin with a mountain of treasure, he wasn't sure what his future held. While Wilhelm loved his country more than anything, he knew his only chance to survive Seeckt's wrath would be to haul a massive fortune back to the capital, enough to fund the Reichswehr's next rebuilding phase and beyond—and do it all before the allies even suspected it was possible. But instead of clutching the seal, Wilhelm wrapped his hand around another drink.

A woman wearing a long evening gown with curly brown locks and crystal blue eyes sat down next to him. Wilhelm glanced at her before turning his focus back to his liquor.

"What's her name?" she asked in English but with a hint of a French accent.

Wilhelm shot her a sideways glance. "She doesn't have a name."

"Yet you're pretty upset you lost her? She must've been a gem."

He shrugged. "That's certainly one way of putting it."

The woman caressed his arm. "There are other women out there."

He waved dismissively. "Not like her."

Under most circumstances, Wilhelm would welcome the woman's advances and at the very least, engage her in a conversation. But he wasn't interested in that kind of conversation tonight. However, she either wasn't getting the message or wasn't satisfied with his response. And Wilhelm found both scenarios unsettling.

He took his glass and got up from his seat, ambling over to a table against the large plate glass window. Through the reflection in the window, he noticed the woman spin around on her stool and walk toward him. She sat in the chair across from him and placed her glass in front of her.

"I'm being as polite as I can," Wilhelm said. "I'm not really interested in your company this evening."

"Fine with me," she said before she reached into her purse and pulled out a gun. "I'm not definitely interested in yours either."

Wilhelm sat upright and raised his hands in a gesture of surrender as he glanced around. Aside from the bartender, the only other person nearby was a man passed out faced down at a table in the far corner. And the bartender was busy drying glasses and putting them away.

"Say a word to him and you'll be dead before he can turn around," the woman said as she situated her purse to shield her weapon from view.

"What do you want?" Wilhelm asked.

She narrowed her eyes. "Where's the seal?"

"The seal?" Wilhelm said. "I don't know what you're talking about. What seal?"

"You know what seal I'm talking about."

"Please," Wilhelm said, "I think it's quite obvious that I don't have it. If I did, would I be here drowning my sorrows over several glasses of brandy? It's gone."

"Where is it?"

"I don't know," Wilhelm said. "And I'm on my way out of the country."

Her eyebrows shot upward. "By going to Mukden?"

"China doesn't exactly have the kind of rail system that always makes sense."

"But you were looking for the seal, weren't you?"

"We were here for other means, but I won't deny that we looked for it, but to no avail. Now, will you put that gun away?"

"Not until I get all the answers I came for."

Wilhelm eyed her carefully. "Who are you?"

"Dr. Thurston Miller's niece. You do remember killing him, don't you?"

He didn't say a word, instead just stared blankly at her. "I'm sorry, but the name doesn't sound familiar to me. How would I know him?"

"You killed him, you monster."

"And why would I do that?" he asked.

"You know good and well why. My uncle, God rest his soul, would never just give out such information willingly. The secret location of the seal of the realm's hidden treasure wasn't the kind of thing he shared with anyone."

"But he shared it with you?"

"Not exactly, but it was in his notebook that you stole from his winter home in France."

Wilhelm shook his head. "I honestly have no idea what you're talking about. I don't know anyone named Dr. Thurston Miller, nor have I been to his winter home."

"It sounds as though you're grieving the death of your uncle and you're quite upset about it. But I can assure you that I had nothing to do with it."

She narrowed her eyes and leaned across the table. "Stop lying to me or, so help me God, I will shoot you."

"No, you won't."

"Don't test me, I'll—"

Dr. Miller's niece collapsed face down on the table after one of the Reichswehr agents slipped up behind her and pistol-whipped her in the head. Wilhelm glanced at the bartender who was intently studying the scene.

Wilhelm stacked a handful of cash on the bar before putting his index finger to his lips. "Don't breathe a word of this to anyone," Wilhelm said. "We were never here."

The man nodded as he tucked the money into his shirt pocket and patted it several times.

"I'm glad we understand each other," Wilhelm said before turning to his soldier. "Take her to the back of the train as discreetly as possible."

Wilhelm followed the man to the back and dumped her unconscious body into the final car of the train, which was nothing more than a place for storage.

"What are we going to do with her, sir?" one of the troops asked.

"We're going to make sure she never becomes a problem again," Wilhelm said.

He scrounged around to find a can of gasoline and used it to drench a rag. Upon securing her to a large chest in the caboose, he stuffed the cloth into the top of the container and eased back onto the platform of the next-to-last car.

Then the door flew open, and Reinhard strode onto the platform. Wilhelm, who was crouching low and holding a box of matches, turned and looked up at his second in command.

"What are you doing?" Reinhard asked. "Have you lost your mind?"

"Quite the contrary," Wilhelm said as he refocused his attention on the matches in his hand and brushed the tip across the side of the box. "I'm incredibly clear on what I'm about to do."

A small flame ignited and Wilhelm held it up, gazing at it for just a moment. He held the fire near the fringe of the rag, which began to burn after a couple of seconds. Then one of his men uncoupled the final car. Wilhelm watched as the caboose slowed to a stop.

A few minutes later, the can of gasoline exploded, rocking the car with Dr. Miller's niece inside. The resulting fire consumed the caboose, but it still remained on the tracks.

"We shouldn't have any more distractions for the rest of this trip," Wilhelm said as he stood and smiled. "Now let's go get that seal and take the treasure home to Berlin."

CHAPTER 32

JUST BEFORE 4 P.M. RICHARD AND HELEN JOINED Ashenden on the platform and awaited the arrival of the train from the west that would take them to Mukden. Richard strolled around for a few minutes, stopping to purchase a newspaper. After taking a seat on a bench, he began to flip through the pages.

"I had no idea you could read Chinese," Helen said as she settled next to him.

Richard chuckled. "I can't, but I needed to do something to relax."

"Looking at columns full of indecipherable symbols hardly seems relaxing."

"Why don't you read it to me?" he said, offering her the paper.

"Of course," she said, returning to the front page.

Her eyes widened as she scanned the headlines.

"What is it?" Richard asked.

"It's nothing," she said.

"Nothing? You look like you've seen a ghost. What does it say?"

"It's just an article about a businessman who was arrested last night for counterfeiting."

Richard eyed her closely. "Do you know this man?"

She sighed and then nodded. "He was the man who

portrayed himself as a government agent."

"And I'm assuming he wasn't?"

"I'd already figured out that much, but not until it was too late. Mr. Shufu even suggested as much, though I didn't want to believe him."

"So this businessman deceived you?"

"His name was Shawn Lee, and he didn't portray himself as a businessman to me. He claimed to be a member of the government. I should've known better, but I didn't have much choice at the time when he boarded my boat near Lantau Island. I was in the middle of scrubbing the deck to clean the blood from the two men I'd just killed."

"He used your guilt against you."

"That's not all. He knew my name as well as Foster's. I thought I could trust the man, but I should've known better, especially since he hinted that he would use his gun if I didn't comply."

"Maybe it was an embarrassing lesson, but you're still here."

"Only by dumb luck."

Richard smiled wryly. "I suppose that means I'm not getting any credit for rescuing you last night."

Helen chuckled. "I haven't decided yet."

"Well, let's just agree to forget about it then. We can leave out that part in our report since you disregarded procedure."

"If I'm being honest with you, I didn't want to tip off Shawn Lee that I was on to him. I knew that if I asked him the verification question, it could put me in jeopardy."

"I can't say I blame you."

Helen stood and paced around the bench. "When a man boards your boat with a gun and a couple of guards and then strongly suggests you work with him, you don't ask questions you don't want to know the answer to."

A whistle echoed through the town, accompanied by two more screeching blasts before the train chugged into the station. Ashenden called for Richard and Helen to join him.

The trio found their seats and settled in for the eighteen-hour long ride to Mukden.

* * *

JUST AFTER LUNCH, Richard was gazing out at the landscape when the train slowed down in the middle of nowhere. The other passengers started to scurry about the cabin, several of them stepping onto the small platform between cars and craning their necks around the corner to see up ahead.

"What is it?" Richard asked Helen.

She held up her finger. "Hold on." She leaned across the aisle, listening in as one of the men described what he saw up ahead.

"There's some kind of problem on the track," she said. "I didn't catch everything."

Moments later, the conductor strode through the car and made an announcement, explaining that they needed to clear the rail line to continue. Richard got out and watched as several men were working with a set of pulleys to leverage what appeared to be a burned-out car off the tracks. He offered to help but was ushered toward his cabin.

As he was about to step aboard, he heard one of the men scream, and all the workers dropped what they were doing and filed inside. The frenetic shouting continued, attracting more passengers outside. Helen was one of them and looked at Richard.

"What is it?" she asked.

"I don't know," he said. "I was about to sit back down, and one of the workers yelled and then everyone ran inside the caboose."

Helen joined him on the ground and ventured toward

the scene along with a few other curious people. She returned a couple of minutes later.

"Well?" Richard asked.

"There was a dead body inside," she said.

"A dead body?" Richard asked. "Do you think—"

"I don't know who it could be. But that doesn't look like any accident I've ever seen."

"I was thinking the same thing," Richard said.

When they reached their seats, Ashenden was leaning back in his seat, his hands clasped in his lap and legs crossed.

"Did you see her?" he asked.

Richard furrowed his brow. "See who?"

"The dead woman in the train," he said.

"No I—how did you—"

Ashenden grinned. "While you were all out distracting the conductor, I exited on the other side and got a good look at her. It was a shrewd diversion. You did mean to do that, didn't you?"

Richard didn't answer.

"Please, sit down," Ashenden said. "There's something else I need to tell you."

Richard and Helen eased down into their seats. Ashenden sat upright and leaned forward, continuing to speak in hushed tones.

"That up there was no accident," he said.

"I can't say it surprises me," Richard said. "The Reichswehr can be ruthless at times."

Ashenden raised his index finger. "If the Reichswehr were the culprits."

"Do you think Shufu could've done this?" Helen asked.

He shrugged. "Or the Japanese."

"The Japanese?" Richard asked. "Are they hunting this seal?"

Ashenden nodded. "Last night, I didn't tell you the entire story, but that cipher you helped me retrieve enabled us to decrypt several messages between a Japanese commander and one of their spies here in China. Apparently, they've been searching for the seal as well, hoping to unearth the treasure and get it out of the country before anyone noticed it was missing."

"If either Germany or Japan amassed a vast fortune for their respective militaries, that could be disastrous," Helen said.

"Exactly, which is why we need to make sure they both fail," Ashenden said. "Though I'm concerned we might not have enough firepower when we eventually confront them."

"In that case, we'll have to beat them with our wits," Richard said.

Ashenden tousled Richard's hair before he withdrew. "You're such an idealistic young lad, but we need to find out what we're up against before we engage anyone."

The steam engine hissed before the wheels started to turn again. The three agents looked out the window as they passed the burned-out car that had been pulled off the tracks.

Richard shuddered as he saw what was left of the caboose. He was certain it was the work of the Reichswehr— and he was also certain Wilhelm wouldn't be so merciful if they crossed paths again.

CHAPTER 33

ILHELM CROUCHED BEHIND A ROCK AND SNEERED as Lu Shufu and a half-dozen men carrying torches approached the Great Wall. Shufu took a few steps back and surveyed the stones, picking his way along in search of something. But whatever he was looking for eluded him.

For miles and miles, the wall flowed atop the hilly contour of the land. But this section was different as a buttressing berm had been removed, creating a much taller portion. From the other side, marauders would've never been able to tell that there was anything unique about it. But on the inside, it stuck out like a sore thumb, befuddling archeologists and architects regarding the sudden break in design. With no plausible explanation, scientists offered theories like it was a punishment for a worker to remove all the dirt and then build the wall. That idea was as good as any given what anyone knew about that ancient era.

But somehow Shufu had figured out what Wilhelm already knew—this odd part of the wall was the entrance to a vault of unimaginable riches.

"Do you want us to attack?" Erich Krause asked. "The men are ready."

Wilhelm held out his hand, palm facing Krause. "Be patient. Let's let them open the door for us if they can. With only one way out, we'll be able to entrap them and eliminate all of Shufu's men, allowing us safe passage to load our ship."

Krause returned to his position to relay the message to the rest of the Reichswehr soldiers.

Wilhelm turned his gaze back toward the scene unfolding in front of him. Shufu barked orders at his men while pacing back and forth in front of the wall. He fell into a pattern of stroking his chin while studying the area, ambling around while muttering to himself, and then snapping his fingers for one of his employees to do something. Whenever his idea failed, he started the cycle all over again.

This went on for over an hour. And with each passing minute, Wilhelm grew more impatient.

"I think it's time to attack," he said to Reinhard.

"Sir, we've come this far," Reinhard said. "We can wait. Besides, what makes you think you'll be able to find the portal to open the vault?"

"Lu Shufu is an idiot."

Reinhard nodded. "You won't get any argument from me there. But Shufu was smart enough to hire some more men for this expedition. And they look more competent than the ones in Hangchow."

"Hard not to be. All those men are dead."

Another ten minutes passed before Wilhelm decided he was done waiting.

"We're moving in," Wilhelm announced.

"Just give it some more time. Once Shufu and his men get inside, it'll be easy for our men to seize control."

Wilhelm shook his head. "If you haven't figured out that nothing we're doing is ever going to be easy, you haven't been paying close attention."

"But once we get the seal, we'll be doing the same thing Shufu is doing right now, walking in circles and trying to figure out a way inside."

"But at least we'll have the seal," Wilhelm said before he signaled to Krause.

Krause led an advance team of three men closer to the wall. Reinhard took four men with him on the other side, forming a kill box. Wilhelm stayed back with the rest of his troops, including two long-range snipers.

With everyone in place, Wilhelm gave the order to begin the attack.

The sound of the first gunshots stunned Shufu's men for a second before they dove to the ground and started scrambling to safety. There was a small area on both sides of the wall for them to take cover, allowing them to shoot around the corner at their attackers.

Shufu's troops hit three of Wilhelm's men, killing two of them. But the shooting quickly subsided when it became apparent that the Reichswehr unit had emerged victorious.

Wilhelm strode triumphantly toward the wall and found Shufu shaking in a fetal position as he faced a small boulder. He clutched the seal in his hand and didn't acknowledge Wilhelm's presence.

"I'm here to take what is mine," Wilhelm said.

Shufu remained focused on the wall. "It's not yours to take."

"It certainly doesn't belong to you."

"This belongs to the people of China."

Wilhelm held out his hand as he crouched next to Shufu. "There are two ways we can do this—the easy way or the hard way. Give me the seal, and I'll make your death quick and painless. Refuse and I can make the last few minutes of your life very painful."

"You forgot about the third way," Shufu said as spun around and slit his own throat.

The jade stone fell out of Shufu's hand and tumbled across the ground before coming to a stop. Wilhelm reached over and collected the seal, jamming it into his pocket.

"You're right," Wilhelm said. "There was a third option, though I didn't even think about suggesting it. But I appreciate you making my life easy."

Shufu gasped for air before falling limp.

Wilhelm laughed and was joined by the rest of his men, except for Reinhard. The Reichswehr leader recognized that his top commander remained somber.

"What's the matter?" Wilhelm said, throwing his arm around Reinhard. "You said it wasn't going to be easy."

"It wasn't," Reinhard said. "We lost two men—and we still have no idea how to break inside."

"That's why I'm sending you on a little errand to find me an archeology professor at Mukden University tomorrow morning. We'll camp out nearby, and once you bring us someone who can get us inside, the real work will begin."

Reinhard furrowed his brow. "The real work?"

"Transporting an enormous vault loaded with treasure back to our boat won't be easy, especially without attracting any attention and raising suspicion."

"I'll find someone," Reinhard said.

Wilhelm handed Reinhard some money. "Go get a hotel room tonight and get yourself cleaned up. You're going to need to look your best in an effort to convince that professor to come with you."

* * *

THE NEXT MORNING, Reinhard pulled his jacket taut before glancing at himself in the mirror one last time. He ran his fingers through his hair and practiced a warm smile. If he was going to get home soon, he needed to be as winsome as possible to convince a Mukden University professor to go on a little excursion.

Upon arriving on campus just before 8:00 a.m., he managed to get someone who spoke just enough English to get pointed in the direction of the archeology department. When Reinhard arrived at the building, he noticed there were only two names listed on the directory. He asked a secretary if either of the men were in, but she furrowed her brow and stared at him.

Just as he was about to begin an expedition down the hallway in search of the professors, a woman with a British accent addressed him from across the room.

"May I help you, sir?" she asked.

Reinhard spun around to see a slender woman with brown hair wearing a dress with a long trench coat. She held a small briefcase in her hand as she looked him up and down.

"I need to speak to an archeology professor," he said.

Her smile widened. "Well, you're already talking with one. How can I help you?"

Reinhard eyed her closely. "Hans Dorman," he said, offering his hand. "And you are?"

"Dr. Barbara Baker," she said as she shook hands with him. "I'm visiting here from Oxford while I do a little research."

"Fantastic," Reinhard said. "If you're looking for something to research, I have a site you might be interested in."

"Well, Mr. Dorman, I hate to disappoint you, but I'm incredibly busy right now. Perhaps next week."

"Oh, no. It—it can't wait."

"In that case, best of luck to you, and I hope you find someone willing to help you."

She turned and strode back down the hallway toward her office. Reinhard hustled after her.

"Don't you at least want to know what I found?" he asked.

She ignored him and kept walking. When she reached her office door, she glanced over her shoulder and realized he was still there.

"You are quite persistent," she said. "But if you'll please excuse me, I have some very important work I need to catch up on before my classes begin later this afternoon."

She slipped inside and tried to close the door, denied by Reinhard's foot, which he wedged against the doorjamb.

"You haven't even heard what I found," he said. "You might want to at least listen to me before rejecting me immediately."

"Mr. Dorman, please, I—"

"Ever heard of the seal of the realm?"

She furrowed her brow. "The heirloom seal of the realm?"

He nodded.

Dr. Baker's eyes widened as she digested the news. "You have this seal in your possession?"

"Not at this exact moment, but I can show it to you."

She took a deep breath before pacing around the room in a circle.

"What is it?" he asked.

"It's just that—oh, I don't want to trouble you with this. It's nothing."

Reinhard stopped her and placed his hands on her shoulders. "Is there something I need to know about the seal?"

She withdrew, breaking his grip on her. Turning her back on him, she stared out the window and remained silent.

"I'm sorry, Dr. Baker," he said. "Maybe this was a mistake coming here."

Reinhard wasn't sure why the doctor was behaving in such a manner, but he could only assume piquing her interest was the only way to get her talking again.

"No, wait," she said. "Don't go. Have a seat and I'll tell you everything."

They both sat down, and Dr. Baker revealed why she'd become so emotional.

"I used to work with Dr. Thurston Miller," she said. "Are you familiar with him?"

Reinhard pursed his lips and nodded slowly. "I believe I've heard the name once or twice before."

"The seal of the realm was his passion, his Holy Grail, if you will. Every opportunity he got to write about or talk about the seal, he would. But he died recently and never got to fulfill that dream."

"Dream of what? Getting his hands on the seal?"

She shook her head. "Finding the seal was one thing, but the seal acted as a key to an enormous fortune hidden somewhere. But you probably already know this, don't you?"

Reinhard shrugged. "I've heard bits and pieces of it here and there. So, would you like to see the seal?"

She gasped. "You have it?"

"Yes, I can show it to you later tonight, if you like."

"No," she said as she stood. "I must see this precious artifact right now."

"What about all your work?" Reinhard asked.

"That can wait. This can't."

An hour later, they approached the wall just outside the city where Reinhard had left Wilhelm and the rest of the Reichswehr troops.

"I asked you to bring me an archeology professor, not a secretary," Wilhelm bellowed.

"She is a professor," Reinhard said. "Just give her a

chance."

Wilhelm introduced himself and chatted with her for a moment before producing the seal from his pocket.

"Is this what you came to see?" Wilhelm asked.

She nodded as her eyes lit up. Taking the seal from Wilhelm, she held it up and examined it in the light.

"Extraordinary," she said. "Where oh where did you find this gem?"

"It's a long story, actually," Reinhard said. "However, we were hoping that you might be able to help us with the next portion of this mystery and open the vault with all the treasure."

"And do you know where the vault is located?" she asked.

Wilhelm gestured toward the wall. "Right here."

Dr. Baker chuckled and then stopped suddenly. "Oh, you're serious. This looks like a brick wall."

"Why do you think I brought you all this way?" Reinhard asked.

"I suppose I thought you wanted to stay well out of sight," she said.

Wilhelm nodded. "We do. Now, are you willing to help us or not?"

She flipped the seal back to him and walked back toward Reinhard's car. "Not. Now, I appreciate the opportunity to see the seal, but I'm more interested in getting back to my work."

Wilhelm pulled out his gun and cocked it. "I suggest you rethink your day and help us open the vault."

"A group of Germans acting suspiciously in China with an ancient artifact I can only assume that you stole from someone else—why would I ever help you?" she said.

"Because I'll kill you if you don't."

"Maybe I could spare a few minutes," Dr. Baker said as she turned around slowly.

"You'll spare as many as you need if you want me to spare your life," Wilhelm said as he jammed the seal into her hands. "Now get to work."

Dr. Baker examined the wall for the next hour, feeling niches and poking her finger in every nook and cranny. Then she came across a small indentation in one of the stones comprising the wall.

As she placed the stone into a small portal, her hands started shaking.

"Are you all right?" Reinhard asked her.

"I'm fine," she said. "Just a little nervous—and scared."

"Let's get on with it, shall we?" Wilhelm said as he marched over to her.

The wall started rumbling, and Dr. Baker along with the entire Reichswehr troops all jumped back.

CHAPTER 34

RICHARD HUNKERED DOWN BEHIND A BOULDER ALONG with Helen and Ashenden as they all watched the Reichswehr unit prepare to enter the vault. Wilhelm appeared jumpy, anxious to get inside and see what fortunes were theirs for the taking. Reinhard kept looking over his shoulder, almost as if he was expecting someone.

Peering through a pair of binoculars, Richard gave a detailed account of what was occurring.

"Just tell me when they're going to open the vault," Helen said. "I don't care that Reinhard looks sullen with sunken cheeks."

"I very much appreciate that level of detail," Ashenden said.

Richard chuckled but kept the glasses glued to his face. "It's because you're not much of a reader, Helen. I'm practicing setting the mood for all those people who care about such things."

"And what are these people called?" she asked.

"Literate."

She bristled at his response. "Are you suggesting that I'm not?"

"Of course I know you can read," Richard said. "But you don't seem to enjoy it."

Helen shrugged. "Contrary to what your little theory says about me, I do love a good mystery."

Richard sighed and set the binoculars aside. "One big mystery is about to be solved."

"And which one is that?" she asked.

"The one about whether or not that seal was actually a key to an enormous treasure."

The ground trembled as a woman jammed the seal into a hole in the wall. Richard resumed watching through his glasses and saw a hole open near the base, revealing a flight of stairs that descended into the ground.

"Would you look at that?" Ashenden said as his mouth fell agape.

Helen shook her head. "It's real all right."

Richard let out a long whistle. "Dr. Miller was right."

"But is there treasure still inside?" Ashenden asked. "That's the real question we want answered."

Before they even had a moment to respond, muffled gunshots rang out from the portal.

"Is that what I think it is?" Helen asked.

"We need to get closer and find out what's going on," Richard said, arising from his crouch.

Ashenden stood as well and put his hand across Richard's chest. "That's not a good idea."

"What do you mean? We're intelligence officers. We thrive on information. And from back here, all I know is that a staircase opened up and leads into the ground. What's inside is what we need to know to make a determination about how to interact with the Reichswehr."

"I say turn the vault into a tomb," Helen said. "Lock them inside and throw away the key."

Richard shook his head. "It's bright and sunny outside today, but you are the embodiment of one dark cloud."

"Don't tell me you wouldn't appreciate seeing those ruthless Germans eliminated."

"Of course I would," Richard said, "but do you remember what Hank said? No international incidents. If we start something, we have no idea what it'll do to the treaty agreements. Everything is tenuous enough as it is, so I don't want to incite another battle."

"That's commendable," Helen said. "I'm here mostly for revenge though against the Reichswehr."

"Are you two finished?" Ashenden asked.

Richard sighed as he sat down, acquiescing to their British colleague's demands.

"You don't need to get up close to know what's really going on," Ashenden said. "If you had been on assignment in Japan as long as I've been, you'd recognize that those gunshots are from Nambu pistols and Taishō 14 machine guns, both of which are utilized exclusively by the Imperial Japanese Army."

"What are you suggesting?" Richard asked. "That we just sit here and wait for the dust to settle?"

Ashenden nodded. "That's precisely what we need to do. Anything else would border on sheer lunacy."

Richard set his jaw and glared at the British spy. "Our job is to make sure that the seal—and now all its subsequent treasure—doesn't fall into the hands of our enemies. I think it's safe to say that both of those military units in there are our enemies."

"Then let one of them do the dirty work for us. You and your American ideals, wanting to ride in on a white horse to vanquish your foes. It's utterly ridiculous."

"Is your plan to sit here and pick them off as they exit the doorway there?" Richard asked.

"Why not? It beats venturing into an unknown situation."

Helen placed her hand on Richard's forearm. "He's

242 | GARRETT DRAKE

right, Richard. From our position here, we can shoot them when they try to exit. They won't be able to stay in there forever."

Richard sighed. "What makes you think they're going to exit through that passageway? The Japanese—or whoever you think is inside—found another entrance, which means it can also be used as an exit."

"But the Reichswehr have no idea that we're here," Ashenden said.

"And if they don't win, the Japanese won't be inclined to lug their loot up a set of steps," Richard said. "It's far more likely that there is some ground-level access tunnel that they found since we know who's been in possession of the seal of the realm."

Ashenden grabbed Richard's bicep. "I understand your angst to set eyes on the battle going on in there, but let's just wait a few minutes before rushing down those steps."

Richard shrugged him off and pushed his way past Ashenden.

"Please don't go, Richard," Helen said.

Richard didn't flinch as he pushed his way past Helen and their English colleague. Once more than arm's length away, Richard turned around.

"This is the moment where action is required," he said. "Otherwise, we might become infamous among spies as the three people who could've prevented the next world war yet did nothing but sit around and watch it happen. That's not how I want to be remembered."

He spun back toward the wall before breaking into a dead sprint, both hands clutching guns.

CHAPTER 35

WILHELM WANTED TO BASK IN THE GLOW OF A room filled with treasure when he descended the secret hidden steps. Instead, he had two seconds to survey the scene before he dove behind a pillar to avoid the hail of bullets raining down on his position from the gunmen below. He jammed his shoulder into a column flanking the stairs and checked his weapon. Glancing back toward the entrance, he watched Reinhard and Krause along with several other men darting back and forth in search of cover. Meanwhile, the expression on Dr. Baker's face transformed from awe to horror in about the time it took for her to recognize the sounds she heard were gunshots.

"How do you want to handle this, sir?" Reinhard asked from the behind the column diagonal to Wilhelm.

"I haven't even had a chance to tell how many there are," he answered.

"There might be ten at the most," Reinhard said. "It's hard to tell. They're dashing about the main chamber down there, and it's not exactly lit well enough."

Wilhelm set his jaw. "How did anyone else get inside?"

"There appears to be a tunnel leading out of here in the far corner of the room."

Bullets whizzed past them, pinging off their stone surroundings. And each time one did, Dr. Baker let out a shriek.

"Tell her to shut up, or I'll shoot her myself," Wilhelm said.

Reinhard relayed the message to the professor, who quaked with fear as she nodded in understanding.

"We have to take these guys out," Wilhelm said. "That treasure is ours, and I'll be damned if we didn't come all this way to have it stolen out from underneath us at the last minute."

Wilhelm peered around the side and steadied his aim. He barely had an opportunity to take in the vast amount of treasure strewn about the room. Treasure chests spilling over with gold coins and goblets, sparkling jewels, and decorative clothing. Everything seemed to shine or sparkle despite the dim torches hanging from the wall around the room and the muted sunlight streaming in through a tunnel.

"At least we know the rumors about the treasure are true," Reinhard shouted as he fired at several of the soldiers below.

Wilhelm observed how the Japanese had devised a system to provide cover for the men attempting to recover items across the room. He realized they were simply returning gunfire in the direction of the Germans without the ability to see much near the upper portion of the chamber.

"They can't see us," Wilhelm told Reinhard. "The next time one of their men makes a run for some of the jewels, don't be afraid to return fire. They're just hoping they hit something."

Reinhard nodded and winked. Moments later, another soldier made a run for it across the floor. His colleagues laying down cover didn't intimidate the Reichswehr since Wilhelm shared his big revelation. Two shots later, the soldier was lying dead facedown in the sand.

"Good work," Wilhelm said. "We only have to do that a few more times."

As the dance continued, some of the Reichswehr troop became more emboldened and stood upright and walked down the steps toward the men. Krause was one of them, who descended into the light and was promptly hit in his shoulders. Two other Reichswehr soldiers behind him weren't as fortunate, suffering fatal blows to the chest. They both tumbled down the stairs, dead before their bodies reached the ground floor.

In one corner of the room, a Japanese soldier stepped out into the open and started shooting as he ran back and forth in a haphazard fashion. His distraction drew the fire of most of the Reichswehr troops, irking Wilhelm. The German leader saw a pair of men lug a chest toward the corridor. When he rose up to take aim, they were gone.

Leaning against the column, he watched Dr. Baker race up the steps toward the entrance. Reinhard made a move to get her but was immediately rebuked.

"Leave her," Wilhelm shouted. "She's not worth it. We have what we came for."

Reinhard didn't argue, darting back toward cover as a bullet hit the ground near his feet.

After a couple of intense minutes engaged in battle, the gunfire halted. Wilhelm eased around the column to inspect the area below where the lion's share of the treasure rested. He wasn't sure the vault was clear, but the only combatants he saw were dead on the ground.

"Krause, take a couple of men down there and secure the area," Wilhelm ordered.

Krause obeyed and after a quick sweep declared the vault safe. Celebratory shouts rose up from the men as they clambered down the steps toward the loot.

"There's no time to revel in our good fortune," Wilhelm said, addressing his entire unit. "The Japanese might not be here at the moment, but they could return and likely in greater numbers. If not, they could very well be plotting an ambush. So, I want that tunnel sealed. The only way anyone will be getting in or out of this place will be with this key. Now, let's get to work."

The men spread out and began gathering rocks to stack near the corridor. As they did, Wilhelm took a seat on the steps to watch everyone work. They worked quickly and covered the tunnel with a large boulder that took eight men to budge. He was enjoying the moment, right up until he felt a cold object jammed into his back.

"Say a word, and you're dead," a familiar voice said in a hushed tone.

* * *

RICHARD NUDGED THE BARREL of his gun as far as it would go into Wilhelm's back. The German general raised his hands in a posture of surrender.

"I'm gonna need that seal," Richard said.

Wilhelm looked down and to his right. "It's in this pocket."

Richard fished out the stone and glanced at it for a moment before securing it. Placing his hand on Wilhelm's shoulder, Richard forced his captive backward a few steps and then stopped.

"Order your men to stop what they're doing and leave," Richard said as he shielded himself from view with Wilhelm's body. "And remember, I understand German."

Wilhelm nodded slowly and addressed his troops. "Change of plans, my wolfsrudel. We need to evacuate the vault immediately."

The soldiers stopped and shot befuddled glances at him.

"Change of plans?" Krause protested. "We just chased

off the Japanese, so we could have this treasure for our country, and now you just want to leave it?"

Richard eased into the light. "Do what he says or you'll all die."

"No, kill him," Wilhelm said.

Richard glanced over his shoulder, catching the eye of his two colleagues. "That wouldn't be a good idea. The tables have turned, and your men are the ones in a kill box now."

One of the soldiers reached for his gun, and a bullet whistled near him, hitting the ground at his feet. He jumped back a few feet and laid down his weapon.

"That's right," Richard said. "If anyone else gets any ideas about being a hero, it'll be the last thing you do on this planet. Place your weapons on the ground and file out of here if you want to live."

Each Reichwehr soldier headed up the stairs, glaring at Richard as they passed by him.

After the last German marched past, Richard led Wilhelm up the steps.

"You're not going to kill me?" Wilhelm asked.

"If I can help it, not today," Richard said. "If it were up to me, you would've been dead a long time ago. But you should be thankful that the orders were to keep you alive—unless you resisted."

When they exited the vault and re-entered the daylight, Richard noticed all the Reichswehr soldiers sprinting away from the area. He smiled as he gave Wilhelm one last shove.

"Go catch them," Richard said. "But don't even think about coming back."

Richard reunited outside with Helen and Ashenden.

"Why can't I shoot them all right now?" Helen asked. "It'd eliminate plenty of our problems. We could toss their bodies in the vault and blame the Japanese."

"That's a suggestion I could get behind," Richard said, "but Foster has been explicitly clear about the need to avoid an international incident. If the Germans have a reason to gain sympathy from the international community, we will be giving them the excuse they need to break the Treaty of Versailles and return to terrorizing the rest of Western Europe."

Helen eased her finger off the trigger and trained the barrel of her gun skyward. "You're always ruining everything. It's always better to ask for forgiveness than permission."

"Perhaps but that's not what we're about here, is it?" Richard replied.

Instead of attempting to appeal to Helen's good sense like Richard did, Ashenden decided a direct approach would be more helpful.

"If you fire on those men, I'll shoot you myself," he said.

"Fine," Helen said, raising her right hand in the air in a gesture of surrender. "I won't try to kill any of those vile men. You have my word."

"Good," Ashenden said. "The last thing anyone wants is an international incident. Like Richard said, it could be the catalyst to ignite a war. Let's make sure we don't do anything to provoke the Germans."

Richard placed the stone in the slot. Then the wall that had opened up to reveal the steps into the vault sank into the dirt, obscuring the portal.

"Let's make sure they leave," Richard said.

The trio marched behind Wilhelm and his men, ushering them back to the dock where the Reichswehr's boat awaited along the river.

"It's time for you to go," Richard said to Wilhelm, who had stopped walking.

Wilhelm stared out across the water. "I'm sure we'll meet again. You've been a worthy adversary. And I'll remember your mercy."

Richard wasn't inclined to listen to Wilhelm's hollow platitudes. The last thing he wanted to do was give the German leader the satisfaction of knowing that there was any mutual admiration.

"If I happen to hold the upper hand next time, I wouldn't count on this same amount of mercy. Next time, I might just be tired of your games and ignore the directive. I would advise you to return to your homeland and stay there."

Wilhelm shrugged. "I go where the treasure maps lead me, and if you must shoot me, then you must."

"Just don't say you weren't warned," Richard said before thrusting Wilhelm off the small ramp and onto the deck of his boat.

Richard waited until the German boat chugged away and disappeared around the bend.

"Ready to go?" Helen asked.

Richard cocked his head to one side. "Ready to go where?"

"To make sure it never happens again," she said. "And we need to act fast before the Japanese return."

Richard nodded and smiled. "We need to make sure no one ever finds that treasure again."

CHAPTER 36

"ARE YOU SURE YOU HEARD CORRECTLY?" RICHARD asked as he scanned the names listed on the directory outside the Mukden University archeology department. He furrowed his brow as he ran his finger down the board.

"I know that's what they called her," Helen said. "It was Dr. Baker. I'd bet my life on it."

"Well, she's not part of the faculty, according to this," Richard said.

"Perhaps we should inquire within," Ashenden said.

The three agents approached the secretary at the front desk. Before they asked her anything, a woman walking down the hallway made eye contact with Richard before she spun on her heels and darted in the opposite direction.

"There she is," Richard said, tapping Helen and pointing at the professor.

They all hustled after her, ignoring the pleas from the woman at the front desk to stop. Halfway down the corridor, they all stopped outside the room she slipped into. Ashenden tried to open it, but it was locked.

Helen hit Richard's arm with the back of her hand. "See," she said, looking at the name placard. "I told you it was Dr. Baker."

"That only solves half of our problem," Richard said.

"Now that we know who she is, we just need to get her to talk to us. Think you can work some of your magic to make that happen?"

She nodded and stepped forward, knocking gently on the door. "Dr. Baker, we'd just like a word with you. There's nothing to be afraid of."

Helen placed her ear to the door.

"Is she going to answer?" Richard asked.

"It's too quiet in there," Helen said. "I think she's gone."

Richard didn't hesitate, dashing down the hall and outside. He raced around the side of the building and saw the window had been left open. Peeking inside, he saw the room was empty. Then he started to search the common area for Dr. Baker. It only took a few seconds before he noticed her walking quickly down a nearby path. He rushed over toward her.

"Dr. Baker, I need to speak with you," Richard said as he hustled to keep pace with her.

"I have nothing to say to you," she said, refusing to look him in the eyes.

"I understand that what you saw at the wall earlier today was terrifying, but you must know that we're trying to make sure such things never happen again."

She bristled as she continued her torrid pace. "I didn't come to China to get killed."

"If you don't help, that might be someone else's fate."

"That's not my problem."

"Of course it isn't, but I'm sure you wouldn't want anyone else to endure what you had to. And if you don't help us put an end to this, there might be others at risk of getting captured and forced to do things against their will, just like you were."

"I'm sorry, but I can't help you."

"Can't or won't?" Richard asked.

Dr. Baker stopped and made eye contact with Richard for the first time. "I'm sure you're well-meaning, Mr. —"

"Halliburton," he said, offering his hand. "Richard Halliburton."

She ignored his polite gesture and continued her response. "Mr. Halliburton, I like to discover things about ancient civilizations by digging in the dirt. And I prefer not to be buried beneath it until my time has come. So, if you don't mind, please leave me alone. I have no interest in involving myself in a spat between treasure hunters."

"Those men are gone for now," Richard said. "And they weren't exactly treasure hunters. They were Germany military looking to amass a fortune by selling all those artifacts. And do you know what they will do with all their profits?"

She shook her head.

"They will start another war. Now, I'm sure you don't want that to happen, do you?"

"Of course not, but why do you need me?"

"Because we need you to tell the local authorities so that the treasure is properly returned to the people of China."

She cocked her head to one side. "Why involve me? Why don't you just tell them yourselves?"

"For one, I thought you might appreciate the credit of finding the seal of the realm," Richard said as he held up the jade-colored stone. "The U.S. government also prefers that we keep a low profile in our overseas activities. If we were the ones who brought this to light, we'd be risking unwanted exposure."

"And what do you think will happen if I tell them about this treasure?"

"News of your discovery will be widespread, and the

Chinese government will secure the artifacts, ensuring that neither the Germans nor the Japanese will be able to turn those items into funds used for evil purposes."

Dr. Baker sighed. "When you put it that way, I don't really have a choice, do I?"

"Not if you're interested in ensuring the history of this great nation remains here and not scattered abroad for profit."

"I suppose that's a noble cause."

"But this isn't something that can wait," Richard said. "It needs to be done immediately."

* * *

AN HOUR LATER, Richard and Helen, accompanied by Ashenden, took turns observing the scene at the wall through a pair of binoculars. A host of local law enforcement officials followed Dr. Baker to the wall, where she could be seen urging everyone to step back. She strode up to the wall and placed the seal in the designated slot. Just as it had before, a portal opened up revealing a set of stairs down into the vault.

"She's in," Richard said, pumping his fist exultantly.

"Then why aren't they going inside?" Helen asked.

"Patience," Richard said. "Just have a little patience."

Richard relayed the events as they unfolded. Dr. Baker and her entourage entered the vault and disappeared. After a half a minute, there was still no sign of them re-emerging.

"No news is good news, I guess," Helen said.

"That's right," Richard said. "As far as I can tell, it appears as if they've uncovered the treasure and are likely discussing a way to transport it."

"Your hearing must be incredible," Ashenden said.

"Like I said," Richard began, "that's what I imagine is likely happening right now."

Moments later, Dr. Baker and the rest of the group

streamed out of the portal and reconvened near the foot of the wall.

"You were definitely using your imagination," Helen said. "I don't have a pair of those fancy binoculars plastered to my face, and I can tell from here that whatever happened in there wasn't something that found Dr. Baker favor with those policemen."

Richard studied the scene as what appeared to be the lead detective waved his arms and shouted angrily at Dr. Baker, who stood still, her head hanging.

The detective became more animated as time passed that he pressed the section of the wall next to the seal, forcing the door to swing back into place. However, just before it did, he snatched the seal out of its spot and hurled it inside the vault. Dr. Baker's hands went up in the air before she fell to her knees and buried her head in her hands. The officer gestured for everyone to follow him, leaving Dr. Baker still on her knees in the dirt.

"We have to go help her," Richard said.

The trio waited until the Chinese officials vanished over the hill before rushing over to Dr. Baker. She hadn't moved, still sobbing in despair.

"Dr. Baker," Helen said as she approached the professor, "what happened?"

She picked her head up and snarled at the three intelligence agents. "What? It wasn't bad enough that you embarrassed me like this, so you had to come and gloat about it?"

"Gloat?" Ashenden asked, his mouth agape. "What on earth are you talking about?"

"The vault," she said, trying to regain her composure, "it was empty."

Richard's eyes widened. "Empty? How is that even possible?"

She shrugged. "I'm beginning to question if there ever was anything in there to begin with. I'm wondering if you aren't part of some cruel scheme by Dr. Phillips to discredit me and assure that I never earn tenure at any university."

Richard placed his hands up in a calming gesture. "Whoa, Dr. Baker, we don't even know who Dr. Phillips is."

She wiped her nose on her sleeve. "I don't believe it. I should've known better."

"I swear on my grandmother's grave," Richard said. "We honestly do not know who or what you're talking about."

"Never mind," she said. "What difference does it make any more? That policeman threw the seal into the vault as it closed. Essentially, it can never be opened again—at least, not without putting the structural integrity of the wall at risk."

"We would never do that to you," Richard said. "There was an enormous fortune inside, and the only people who knew about it left Mukden."

"I think it's obvious that someone else knew about it," Dr. Baker said. "Either that or you're lying."

"No one else knew, I swear," Richard said.

"Then this little triumvirate of yours has a leak," Dr. Baker said before rising to her feet and storming away.

Richard started to go after her, but Ashenden grabbed his colleague by the arm. "Just leave her. She would never believe our explanation anyway. It's one of the drawbacks of being in this profession."

Rain started to fall from the sky, adding an extra chill to the air.

Richard shook his head as he watched her walk away. Something had gone terribly wrong—and he wasn't sure who had possession of the treasure.

* * *

THE NEXT MORNING, Richard walked Helen to the train station. She was headed to Peking to meet with the U.S. ambassador and several Chinese emissaries regarding a series of developments in the South Pacific that many officials in the region found disconcerting. And Richard had business elsewhere.

Once the whistle blew, the conductor strolled along the platform and warned passengers that boarding was about to be completed.

"I'm sorry we didn't finish the job the right way," Richard said.

Helen shrugged. "Who's to say we didn't? The Japanese made off with a handful of the treasure, while the Germans didn't get anything. I'd say we did a pretty good job considering the circumstances."

"Or maybe one of them looted the vault and is about to have everything they need to strengthen their military."

"I wouldn't count on that, but we can be as ambiguous about it as we like in our report. I'm sure Foster won't get too bent out of shape about it."

The whistle blew again and the conductor demanded all tickets be turned over to him immediately for anyone intending to make the trip to Peking.

Helen sighed. "It's been a pleasure working with you. Maybe our paths will cross again sometime soon."

"I'd be delighted if that happened," he said.

Richard handed Helen her bag and she turned and climbed aboard. The train hissed before the wheels started to turn. The conductor scrambled a few more passengers aboard as the locomotive started to leave the station.

That's when something—more like someone—caught Richard's eye.

No, it can't be.

Richard rushed toward the next to last car where he saw a familiar face smiling and waving at him. The man winked at Richard and mouthed two words very clearly: "Thank you."

Richard shook his head in disbelief, questioning if his eyes were playing tricks on him.

"I saw you die," Richard said as he approached the window.

Lu Shufu grinned and shrugged. "Never underestimate the power of a good theatrical performance and some well-administered stage makeup."

Richard couldn't do anything about the Chinese antiquities dealer's sudden discovery of a vast treasure. But in the end, it didn't matter. Shufu's moment of glory meant that neither the Reichswehr nor the Japanese escaped Hangchow with the ancient fortune, and that was what mattered most.

Once Richard reached the end of the platform, he stopped and smiled. He could deem his mission a success—and so could Lu Shufu.

CHAPTER 37

Hong Kong

RICHARD MADE THE LONG TRIP TO HONG KONG WITH Ashenden the following day. The British agent was more well-funded than Richard and purchased a private cabin for the train ride, enabling the two men to discuss their missions more freely. However, Richard was most interested in discussing his ambitions as an author.

"You'll certainly have plenty of fodder for your travels," Ashenden said.

"That is a fact," Richard said, "but I'm afraid I won't be able to write about any of this. People want to get lost in adventure in lands far away, but I don't think this is the kind of stories that readers would find believable."

"Why does it have to be true?"

Richard shrugged. "I don't know. I always imagined myself as a travel writer."

"Why limit yourself? There are scores of genres to write in—and almost all of them would welcome someone with as much experience traveling the world as you have."

"That's definitely something to consider, though I'm already hard at work on my first book. Maybe if that one doesn't work out, I'll try some other styles."

"Whatever you write, I'll look forward to reading it," Ashenden said. "I fancy myself as quite the reader."

With that, Ashenden reached into his bag and produced a novel.

"What are you reading?" Richard asked.

"Of Human Bondage by W. Somerset Maugham," Ashenden said. "I hear it's one of his best."

When the train finally reached Hong Kong, Richard and Ashenden were greeted on the platform by Hank Foster and George Gentry, the head of British intelligence in East Asia and the Pacific regions.

"Gentlemen, we need a word with the two of you," Foster said, gesturing toward the exit.

They walked to a restaurant on the other side of the street from the station and settled into their chairs around a round table in the back.

"What's this all about?" Richard asked.

"George, would you like the honors?" Foster asked.

Gentry nodded as he filled his pipe with tobacco. When he was finished, he lit up and took a couple of puffs before continuing.

"Based on all the reports we've received from your joint mission, we believe you might just be the right tandem for an operation that requires two resourceful agents," Gentry said. "As we discussed this possibility, we both agreed that the agent we had best suited for this assignment was already in this region."

Richard crinkled his brow and cocked his head to one side. "You do realize that we didn't get the treasure from the heirloom seal's vault, don't you?"

Foster nodded. "And you obviously haven't seen the newspapers, have you?"

He slid a copy of that day's paper across the table so the two agents could see it. "It's this afternoon's edition of *The Hongkong Telegraph*," Foster said. "Look just below the fold."

Richard's eyes scanned the page until he noticed the headline that Foster was referring to.

"How did this happen?" Richard asked.

"Does it really matter?" Ashenden replied. "We did succeed after all."

Richard re-read the headline aloud: "Hangchow Antiquities Dealer Arrested for Theft of Dynasty Treasure."

Richard shook his head in disbelief. "How did they—"

Foster winked. "Sometimes these things just happen and there's no real explanation for it."

"I'd say that you gentlemen handled this situation in this best possible manner under some of the worst possible conditions," Gentry said. "You were thrown the unexpected twist of having to deal with not one by two nefarious units. And the two of you along with Helen managed to outwit them to the point that now all that treasure is going to be owned and displayed by the Chinese government. But most importantly, it's not in the hands of the Germans or the Japanese."

"I'm not sure we deserve that much credit," Richard said. "It's not like we fought them all off like some swashbuckling pirates."

"Exactly," Foster said. "There are times when you need to plow your way through, and there are other times when you need to use your wits. And when you venture into enemy territory, agents who act with discretion not only survive but, more often than not, succeed."

"So, where are we headed?" Ashenden asked.

"It's back to Japan for you," Gentry said. "We figured since Richard here was so helpful in securing the cipher, you two might be able to handle a very sensitive assignment there."

"What exactly do you want us to do?" Richard asked.

Gentry reached into his briefcase and produced a folder. "All the pertinent details are in there," he said, patting the table. "Your ocean liner leaves in the morning from here. The tickets are inside."

Richard scooped up the documents. "You are aware that I don't speak Japanese, right?"

Gentry nodded. "You'll have a few weeks on the boat to figure it out. Your fellow agent here will make a fine tutor."

"Good luck, gentlemen," Foster said as he stood. Gentry joined him, and the two men strode out of the restaurant.

"Well, I've always wanted to go to Japan," Richard said.

"It's an extraordinary place," Ashenden said.

"So I've heard. I figured it'd be a great place to visit for my travel book." Richard paused and eyed Ashenden closely. "Have you ever considered writing?"

Ashenden shrugged with a wry smile. "The thought has crossed my mind."

"What would you write about?"

"I'd probably write about something I know, maybe disguise my life experiences in a novel."

"That would be most interesting," Richard said.

"Probably not as interesting as what's inside that envelope. Ready to open it?"

Richard nodded and broke the seal. His eyes widened as he scanned the first page.

"This ought to be fun," he said.

Ashenden looked at Richard and winked. "Absolutely."

EPILOGUE

WINSTON CHURCHILL STROKED HIS CHIN AS HE READ the last few pages of the manuscript. He grunted as he perused the final story, tapping his cane on the floor. When he was finished, he looked up at the man seated on the opposite side of the desk.

"So, what do you think?" the man asked.

"This is quite the tale," Churchill said. "In fact, it's too close to the truth."

"It is the truth," the writer replied.

"That's why I have a problem with it. You can disguise this as fiction, but there will be more than enough people who will recognize several of these stories no matter how you attempt to cloak your identity."

"Most of those people are dead."

"But not all of them. And I'd prefer not to have the British intelligence agency brought under extra scrutiny. There are already enough foreign entities who despise our methods."

"There's nothing wrong with our methods."

"Of course not, but once the story begins to circulate that we operate illegally in foreign lands, it could create problems for us when it comes to negotiating trade deals and other agreements. I'd rather err on the side of safety."

"As you wish, sir. Just give me a list of the stories you want struck."

Churchill scribbled down a quick list and handed it to the man.

"Is this all of them?" he asked.

Churchill nodded and then held his index finger in the air. "Wait, there's one more."

"Which one is that?"

"I'd prefer that you eliminate the story about the heirloom seal of the realm, Mr. Maugham. We don't want the Chinese government to start dismantling the Great Wall because of your story."

"Consider it done," Maugham said.

Churchill flashed his trademark peace sign and smiled. "Cheerio, Ashenden."

THE END

ACKNOWLEDGMENTS

This project has been incredibly exciting and fun to embark upon, mixing fiction with fact. And quite frankly, none of it would've ever come about without my wife's introduction of Richard Halliburton to me through his timeless Book of Marvels. My children also played a huge role in convincing me to write something about Halliburton after they read his books and would regale me with his stories everyday until I finally decided I needed to read them for myself.

I'd like to thank Rhodes College and Bill Short for allowing me access to Richard Halliburton's archived journals and other material that helped fill in the blanks about what kind of man Richard really was and where he really went. Bill was an incredible help in gathering the information for me and graciously allowing me to plod my way through the material I requested. Without Bill's assistance, I'm not sure this project would've ever become a reality—at least in my lifetime.

Sir Richard J. Evans also enthusiastically aided the creation of this story in giving me plausible creative ways to weave the storyline of the Reichswehr into this fictionalized tale. I'm so grateful that when I reached out to him that he was more than gracious in supplying me with ample fodder—material that will be used in future novels in this series.

And as always, this book wouldn't be what it is without Krystal Wade's skillful editorial direction. She made this book much better than when I originally conceived it.

John Pirhalla has been incredible to partner with in creating the audio version of this book, and I look forward to his voice being the one that shares many more Richard

Halliburton tales in the future.

And last but certainly not least, I'm most grateful for you, the reader, who decided to invest your time with one of my stories. I hope you had as much fun reading this book as I did writing it.

MORE RICHARD HALLIBURTON ADVENTURES

Made in the USA
Las Vegas, NV
16 October 2024

96933693R00156